THE LAST
REVOCATER

BOOK FIVE OF THE STAR
SCAVENGER SERIES

G J OGDEN

ISBN-13: 978-1-8380226-1-7

Cover design by Grady Earls
Editing by S L Ogden

www.ogdenmedia.net

THE STAR SCAVENGER SERIES

One decision can change the course of an entire civilization. One discovery can change your life...

READ THE OTHER BOOKS IN THE SERIES:

- Guardian Outcast
- Orion Rises
- Goliath Emerges
- Union's End
- The Last Revocater

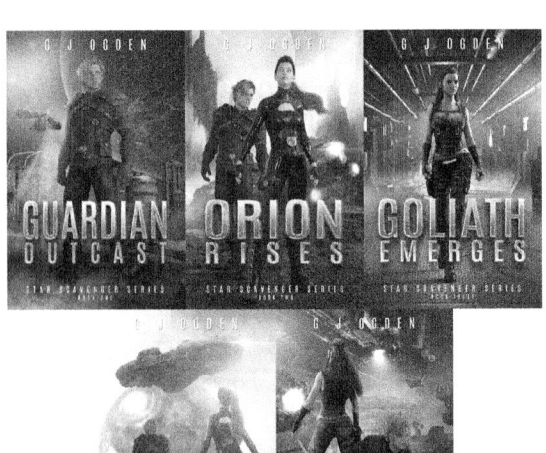

ACKNOWLEDGMENTS

Thanks to Sarah for her work assessing and editing this novel, and to those who subscribed to my newsletters and provided such valuable feedback.

And thanks, as always, to anyone who is reading this. It means a lot. If you enjoyed it, please help by leaving a review on Amazon and Goodreads to let other potential readers know what you think!

If you'd like updates on future novels by G J Ogden, please consider subscribing to the mailing list. Your details will be used to notify subscribers about upcoming books from this author, in addition to a hand-selected mix of book offers and giveaways from similar SFF authors.

Subscribe for updates:
http://subscribe.ogdenmedia.net

Other series by G J Ogden:

- The Planetsider Trilogy
- The Contingency War Series

PROLOGUE

Unable to watch any longer, the Telescope turned its eye away. Through the gift and curse of its boundless vision – the masterpiece of its Corporeal creators – it had observed the ruination of yet another planet, and yet more thousands of corporeal lives. More victims of the wrathful might of Goliath.

It had seen all this happen before. Millennia ago, it had witnessed countless billions die, as the Revocater fleet failed to temper Goliath's rampage of destruction. Then, the great ship had limited its assault to sentient organic life, but this time Goliath's callousness knew no bounds. This time, all it left behind in its wake was rock and dust.

For a long time, the Telescope had watched Goliath in its forced exile, drifting aimlessly through space, lost and rudderless. For a long time, it had observed the corporeal offspring of the creators in System 5118208 evolve and grow. It had always thought them beyond the reach of Goliath. It had always thought them safe, and that they, along with the Telescope, would be a lasting legacy of the Corporeals. Then the human seed species discovered the first portal, and the Telescope knew it would only be a matter of time before Goliath caught their scent. Time had been one of the few building blocks of the universe that the Corporeals had never mastered. Like Goliath, the march of time was relentless and inescapable. Now, at last, time had caught up with them all.

Yet there was still a chance. The last Revocater had survived. This lone warrior had prevailed where all the others of its kind had failed. Like Goliath, the last Revocater was a unique entity, with a singular purpose. Both were cunning and powerful, but this time the last Revocater had something it did not have the first time it faced Goliath – it had allies.

The human corporeal seed race was fragile and flawed, but they possessed a determination equal to that of the great ship. The Telescope had watched their struggle, as it watched them now, split between the Corporeals' home world and the planet the humans called Mars. One party battled to secure the prototype Revocater, while the other fought to secure the crystal – the only weapon that would end Goliath's advance.

The Telescope knew that the odds were still against them, but it trusted the last Revocater to know what was best. It had defeated Goliath once before, and it had to do it again. Because if it failed to stop the great ship, then the last corporeal seed-species in the galaxy would be exterminated. And this time, Goliath would ensure that nothing remained to suggest that organic, sentient life had ever existed at all.

CHAPTER 1

The fight to secure the underground facility where the prototype Revocater lay hidden had been won; but it had not come without cost. Tobin Rand was far from the first victim of Goliath's rage, and Liberty knew he would not be the last. However, she wasn't giving up on him. They still had a long way to go, and Liberty was determined that they would all make the journey together. Too much had been lost already.

Morphus had carried the unconscious and gravely injured body of Tobin Rand onto the dorsal hull of the Revocater. All the while, the entity had continued to apply pressure to the vicious wound that the seed drone had inflicted to Tobin's chest. This, and his own will to survive, was all that was keeping the young man alive.

Morphus had also not escaped the conflict unscathed. Liberty could see that the damage the alien AI had sustained during the fight with the seed drones had weakened it too. However, the entity, which still maintained its female form, had continued on without complaint or requests for assistance. Liberty had wanted to help Morphus, but her own body was still drained of almost all its vitality. Simply keeping up with the entity as it moved across the glacial surface of the titanic vessel was physically tortuous. Liberty felt helpless and useless. More than that, she felt a sickening worry and guilt that Tobin's injuries were beyond Morphus' skill to heal.

After making their way across the outer hull of the Revocater for what felt like hours, Morphus opened a doorway and led them inside. It then single-handedly hauled Tobin through the vast complex of hexagonal corridors, like a herculean Jean Valjean, dragging Marius through the sewers of Paris. Eventually, they reached what looked like a large bulkhead, with seemingly no way through. Morphus approached the wall, Tobin still at his side, and pressed its hand to the metal. An iris-like opening appeared and then widened enough for them all to get through.

Liberty went inside last, entering into a hexagonal room that was roughly the same size as a basketball court. It reminded her of the cockpit inside Morphus' shuttle, only expanded to a much larger scale.

Morphus moved further inside the room, and then lay Tobin down on the floor. A platform rose up out of the metal deck, lifting Tobin onto it like a mortuary table. Then metal plates that shimmered with the same lustrous glow as Liberty's augmented skin surrounded the young man's body. Eventually, the plates covered his wound, and Liberty saw Morphus withdraw its makeshift bandage from Tobin's chest. It stepped away, then the end of Morphus' arm transformed back into a human hand. Blood dripped from Morphus' fingers onto the deck and Liberty looked away. She'd been selfish to want Tobin to come with her. If anything happened to him now, it would be her fault.

"Is he going to be okay?" Liberty wheezed, practically collapsing onto the floor beside the table. She felt like she'd just completed an arduous climb to the summit of a mountain, where the thin air made it difficult to recover her strength.

"His injuries are still life-threatening," replied Morphus, with all the bedside manner of a rock.

Liberty slumped to the flat of her back and held her aching head. "Just tell me you can save him," she said. Then before Morphus could reply, she added, "Even if you don't know that you can; just tell me something to give me hope, Morphus." She lifted her head a little to look at the entity, though even this small movement required a gargantuan effort. "You do understand hope, don't you?"

Morphus' synthetic brow furrowed a little as it worked on the strange bed-like contraption that Tobin had been ensconced in. "The Corporeals that created me programmed me with knowledge of this concept you call hope," said Morphus. "I did not understand it at that time. I am trying to understand it better now."

"That's good," replied Liberty, encouraged that there was more to Morphus that the detached clinicality of numbers. However, Morphus did not appear to be encouraged by Liberty's enthusiasm. Instead it appeared sullen and contemplative.

"The Corporeals hoped that Goliath had not become the thing they feared. They hoped they had not made a terrible mistake in creating it. And when it became clear that they had, they hoped that the Revocater fleet could defeat it." Morphus continued to make some adjustments to the table, then moved over to the side wall. Glancing back at Liberty with its artificial, analytical eyes, it added, "Hope was not enough to save the Corporeals then, and it will not be enough to save us now."

Managing to muster enough strength for another short burst of movement, Liberty hauled herself up, and sat, cross-legged. "But you did defeat Goliath," she said. "And if Hudson and I hadn't found that damn crystal, it would still be lost, somewhere on the other side of the galaxy. Hope may not be a strategy, but it was hope that created you, and it was you alone that defeated Goliath, and saved Earth. Hope can be powerful, Morphus, don't you see? Hope matters."

Morphus pressed its hand to the wall, and Liberty watched as it began to glow and morph into the alien metal. Seconds later, lights started to flicker on all around the room. Then, from somewhere deep inside the belly of the ship, there was a rumble. It was as if the titanic vessel was a starving giant waking from a long sleep. When Liberty finally looked back at Morphus, it was standing in front of her. The alien entity crouched low, and met Liberty's eyes.

"Hope alone will not help the Tobin Rand entity," it said, with an unusual softness to its synthetic voice. Liberty's eyes fell to the cold metal deck, but Morphus had not finished speaking. "But I promise you that I will do everything in my power to save his life. It is my purpose, Liberty Devan entity. To protect corporeal life is why I was created. It is the only reason I exist. At the moment, the Tobin Rand entity is stable. He is strong, in body and in mind. And, if it comforts you to know, it is my sincere hope that he will survive. That is all the hope I am capable of offering you right now."

Liberty met Morphus' strange alien eyes again, before smiling and managing a tired nod. In many ways she appreciated the alien's honesty. False hope was no better than a lie, and if Tobin was going to die, she'd rather know it and face it now.

Though Morphus had given no assurances that it could save Tobin, its pledge that it would do all it could was enough for Liberty.

In her short life, much of which had been spent on the streets, Liberty had experienced far more of the darker side of humanity than the virtuous. Wa few notable exceptions, little had happened in the recent chaotic and exciting weeks since becoming a relic hunter to change her outlook. However, Morphus had been a rare beacon of light. Liberty doubted that she would meet a more noble being, if she lived to be a hundred.

"Speaking of protecting corporeal life," groaned Liberty, as she hauled herself to her feet, assisted by Morphus. "I don't suppose this Revocater has a kitchen, or even just a fridge I could raid? I'm starving!"

Morphus frowned. "My analysis of your body chemistry suggests you are nutrient and energy deficient, but you are far from the point of starvation. And I fail to comprehend how conducting a military operation on a refrigeration unit will abate your hunger?"

Liberty laughed weakly and shook her head, "It's just a turn of phrase, Morphus. It just means I could really use something to eat right now."

Morphus nodded, and began walking towards the far end of the hexagonal space, inviting Liberty to follow. "I am afraid that I do not have a kitchen, or a fridge for you to 'raid'," it said. Liberty noticed that the end of the room was reconfiguring itself as they approached. "But this planet contains a wide variety of biota. I will collect some as we depart, and use them to synthesize various nutrient-rich chemical compounds that will help to sustain your corporeal form."

Liberty raised an eyebrow, "Sounds delicious..."

They reached the area at the end of the room, and Liberty realized it had been configured to resemble the flight controls of the Orion. It was similar to the way Morphus had modified its shuttle, except this time, due to the additional space, it had created a rudimentary living area too. It was like a combination of the living space on the Orion, with its semi-circular couch, and the bunk in Liberty's quarters.

"You may rest here," said Morphus. "The Revocater will require some time to reach full power, during which time I will conduct repairs to my own physical form. And I also wish to run diagnostics to ensure this vessel is still functioning within norms."

Liberty practically collapsed onto the recreation of her bunk. It felt like lying on a bed of tire rubber, but she was so exhausted that she didn't care. "Don't forget my dinner," she called out, closing her eyes.

"As a temporary measure, I will deliver some glucose and other nutrients intravenously," replied Morphus, as a pod rose out of the deck just behind the flight consoles. Liberty's eyes sprang open and she scowled at Morphus, before the entity quickly added, "With your permission."

Liberty sighed and relaxed back on the bed again. "The way I feel right now, I'll take anything you can offer."

"Very well," said Morphus. Then, unseen by Liberty, it transformed out of its female form, and flowed into the pod, like molten gold.

A few minutes later, tubes rose out of the makeshift bed and wrapped themselves around Liberty's wrist. However, Liberty didn't recoil at their touch, because she had already fallen asleep.

CHAPTER 2

Liberty woke with a start and pushed herself upright on the replica bed that Morphus had created. The sudden movement made her dizzy, and for several seconds she was disoriented. It was dark, like at sunset, and at first, she thought she was in her bunk on the Orion, but something about where she was didn't make sense. Then a thin tube suddenly unwrapped from around her wrist, and slid off underneath the bed.

"It's a snake!" she yelped. Liberty jumped off the bed and darted back, before bumping into a solid mass. She yelped again, but then saw that the mass was, in fact, Morphus. She noticed that the entity's entire body was subtly shimmering in the low light.

"Very curious, there should be no elongated, legless, carnivorous reptiles on this planet," said Morphus, wearing an inquisitive frown. It was peering over to where Liberty had been looking.

The light level then increased and Liberty finally remembered where she was. "You scared the hell out of me," she said, after managing to wrestle back control of her wits.

"I apologize if I startled you," replied Morphus, "I trust you are well-rested?"

Liberty stretched her neck muscles and flexed her arms a little, noting that the feeling of stiffness had gone. "Yes, I do feel better, actually, thanks," she said, before her eyes fell on the strange bed-like contraption that Morphus had placed Tobin inside. There seemed to be even more tubes and wires protruding from both Tobin and the device he was attached to. Liberty's face fell, and Morphus seemed to sense her concern.

"Do not be alarmed, the Tobin Rand entity is currently stable," said Morphus, as they both walked up beside the bed. When they got closer, Liberty could see that some of his body was now covered by shimmering metal panels.

"How is he?" asked Liberty, resting a hand on his forehead. His skin felt cool to the touch.

Morphus moved to the opposite side of the bed to where Liberty was standing. She noticed that the alien entity's own damage appeared to have been repaired. It was in its usual female form, but there were no longer any patches of smooth metal. The illusion of skin, hair and clothes was complete again. If anything, Morphus looked even more human than ever.

"I have placed the Tobin Rand entity in a coma while the injuries are being repaired," Morphus said. "It has been necessary to partially augment his musculoskeletal structure, where the damage was most extensive."

Liberty took her hand off Tobin's head and gently squeezed his hand instead, before glancing up at Morphus. "Can you say yet whether he'll pull through this?" She almost immediately regretted asking the question. Given the entity's tendency towards brutal honesty, she almost dreaded the response. However, Morphus' answer caught her completely off guard.

"I remain... hopeful," Morphus said, offering what Liberty could only have described as a reassuring smile.

"That's good enough for me," Liberty replied, smiling back at the entity. Then there was a dull thud that seemed to echo distantly through the hull. Liberty scowled, "What was that?"

Morphus turned to the end wall, in front of the flight controls it had created previously, and held up its hand. The wall switched to show the surface of the planet.

"Is that where we are?" asked Liberty, and Morphus nodded. "But how can you see this?"

"This image is actually relayed from the Telescope," Morphus replied. "It sees everything. But this is not what I wanted you to look at."

The image then zoomed in on what appeared to be dozens of seed ships and seed drones. Liberty moved closer to the screen and watched as some of the seed drones burrowed into the ground. Rock and soil then exploded upwards, and Liberty again felt another distant shudder vibrate through the ship.

"They're trying to blast their way in here?" asked Liberty, looking back at Morphus.

Morphus nodded, "That is correct." The image on the wall then zoomed out again, and Liberty could now see other explosions popping off across a wide expanse of land. These were closely followed by more rumbles, echoing through the hull. "The destruction of the surface structures by Goliath, thousands of years ago, buried this complex under millions of tons of rock and soil," Morphus continued. "But they will soon breach the outer bay doors, and once inside they will resume their attempts to cripple the Revocater."

Liberty's pulse had barely had chance to slow, before she felt it rapidly quickening again. "Can we get out, before they reach us?"

"Yes, but I will need your assistance," said Morphus, indicating towards the pilot's chair. "I had hoped there would be time to run through some simulations before you began to pilot the Revocater. But I am afraid we are out of time."

Liberty stepped up to the chair and looked at the panels and instruments. Her own, admittedly limited piloting knowledge, plus the knowledge that Morphus had implanted into her brain, came flooding back. However, she also recognized that there was a world of difference between knowing how to do something, and actually doing it.

Liberty sat in the chair and tentatively took hold of the flight column, which was an exact replica of the one on the Orion. The metal began to give off a subtle luster, like Liberty's skin. She could actually feel a connection to the ship that went far beyond the mere tactile feel of the controls. It was like the Revocater was somehow an extension of her senses, but it was like nothing she had ever experienced before.

"What do I do?" asked Liberty, glancing back at Morphus with the frightened expression of someone about to take their driving test.

"You will know what to do," replied Morphus, moving back to the pod just behind the flight controls. "You have a natural affinity for the language of machines and technology. Simply trust your instincts." Morphus then flowed back into its pod, and Liberty could hear the thrum of the Revocater's reactors and engines building. It was a sound unlike anything she'd heard before, and was at once both fearsome and electrifying.

"I will now open the bay doors," came the disembodied voice of Morphus, "then you will take us out, and rise into orbit."

"That simple, huh?" muttered Liberty, as she tried to force her breathing into a more regular, controlled rhythm.

"Are you ready?" asked Morphus.

Liberty nodded in a rapid, staccato fashion. Though the gesture was more an attempt to gee herself up for the task than it was a response to Morphus' question.

Liberty looked at the wall in front of her, wishing that she could see more of a panoramic view around the ship. Then, as if responding to her thoughts, the image changed. She could not only see directly ahead – currently just the end wall of the hangar – but above and to the sides too. It was more than just a visual awareness, though, Liberty realized. She also instinctively knew the distances from the hull to the walls surrounding her, like sensing an object touching the hairs on her skin. Then she looked down and wished she hadn't done. The floor beneath her feet was showing a view directly downwards. It was like her pilot's chair was floating in mid-air. And while this undoubtedly gave her great visibility, it was also more than a little alarming.

Suddenly light filtered in from above her head, and she looked up to see the complex's massive bay doors opening. Rock and rubble rained in on the Revocater, like house-sized hailstones, but they just bounced harmlessly off the alien hulk's hull. Mixed in with the rubble, she could also see seed drones falling inside the hangar. Except now there wasn't anyone outside to help clean them off.

"Morphus, what about the drones landing on the hull?" Liberty called out, "There's nothing to stop them cutting through!"

"I will deal with the seed drones," came the alien entity's confident reply. "The bay doors are now fully opened. You have control."

The words cut through her like a hot knife through butter. "I have control... I have control..." she repeated, her voice anxious and breathy. She then tightened her hold on the controls, and peered up. The contrast between the peaceful, clear blue sky and the storm of emotions raging in her body was stark, but it gave her something to reach for.

Sucking in another deep lungful of air, she let it out slowly, then began to raise the mighty Revocater from the berth it had rested in for thousands of years.

Liberty could feel the movement of the ship as if it were her own body. However, the effort needed for her to maintain control was like trying to wade through deep sea water, while strong tides pulled her back and forth under the surface. The Revocater veered to starboard, smashing into the wall and crushing the floors upon floors of balcony walkways. Liberty wrestled the controls to port and the ship responded, but the physical strength required was more than she had anticipated. More rock and wreckage fell onto the ship, as the ground above them was shaken by the powerful collisions. Liberty held tightly onto the controls. *Trust yourself... You can do this!* she thought, willing herself on. The Revocater responded to her commands and continued to rise.

Liberty sucked in another gasp of air, realizing that she'd been holding the last one since the ascent began. The ship then lurched forward, smashing into the end wall, but it continued to rise, gouging out a huge furrow into the perimeter of the complex. She eased the Revocater back, beginning to get more of a feel for the ship's size. It was like driving a truck compared to driving a two-seater sports car. The basic mechanics of operation were similar, but the reality was worlds apart.

The Revocater pulled away from the end wall and Liberty finally managed to center its ascent. She was growing in confidence now almost as quickly as the ship was gaining altitude. The recreation cockpit was then bathed in light as the Revocater rose up above the surface of the planet, like a humpback whale leaping out of the water.

The sensation of floating in mid-air suddenly became disorienting, and Liberty's head began to spin. The momentary distraction caused her to again veer off to starboard, towards what remained of one of the Corporeals' great cities. Groaning with effort, she tried to turn the enormous hulk away, but she was unable to stop the massive ship from smashing through the remains of what were once titanic skyscrapers. The buildings shattered and fell, like they were nothing more than icicles that had been struck with a crowbar. Liberty could even feel the impacts against her skin, like snowflakes landing on her face in a winter storm.

Head pounding and muscles burning, Liberty eventually regained control, and climbed the ship higher and higher. With the immediate threat of crashing behind her, Liberty breathed an audible sigh of relief. However, her thoughts then turned to the seed drones, and the threat they still posed to the ship.

A section of the wall ahead of her changed to show a view along the surface of the vessel's outer hull. It was again as if the Revocater had read Liberty's mind. She could see some of the seed drones still attached, but steadily each was blasted by a surge of energy from the hull. Morphus appeared to be electrifying the alien metal, and exterminating the drones, like a bug zapper killing flies.

With the danger from the seed drones seemingly under control by Morphus, Liberty's confidence swelled. The effort of controlling the mighty ship continued to diminish as her enthusiasm grew. And as the Revocater punctured the veil of blue sky and passed into the darkness of space, she was actually starting to enjoy herself.

"We made it!" Liberty called out. "This ship is incredible."

"You have done well, Liberty Devan entity," said Morphus. However, instead of the voice surrounding Liberty, as it had done before, it came at her directly from her right. She looked over and jumped with fright as she saw Morphus sitting in the second seat.

"You scared the hell out of me!" said Liberty, before adding with more emphasis, "again..."

"I apologize," said Morphus, before replicating Liberty's mannerisms, and adding, "again..." Liberty didn't know whether it was trying to be amusing, or merely imitating her, but It served to make Morphus appear a touch more human. "However, I thought it might be more comfortable for you if I retained a physical form," the alien entity continued.

Liberty then noticed there was something strange about how Morphus was sitting. She looked more closely and realized that the entity was actually physically connected to the seat, as if they were one solid piece.

"In order to manage the Revocater's systems, I must remain a part of it," said Morphus. It was as if the alien had read her mind, just as the ship had seemed to also react to her thoughts. She released the controls, and the lustrous glow of the metal faded. "Are you in my head?" she asked, scowling at Morphus.

"Not any longer, since you have released the controls," replied Morphus.

Then the Revocater began to shudder, as if it were an old-fashioned commercial airliner that had hit a patch of turbulence. Liberty instinctively grabbed the controls again; they glowed in harmony with her skin, and the ship stopped shuddering.

"You must tell the Revocater to hold its course, before releasing the controls," said Morphus, answering the question that Liberty was just about to ask. "You can think of it as a sort of autopilot. But one that you program with your mind, rather than a computer console."

Liberty nodded, but then realized she had no-idea where they were supposed to be going. "How do I know what course to set?"

Morphus didn't answer, and as Liberty glanced across to the second seat, the entity appeared to have frozen. Then Liberty felt something, as if a bug was crawling on her skin. As she turned her thoughts to the sensation, the image ahead of her switched to show a view to their rear. The Corporeals' planet was slowly sinking into the distance, and there was also a series of energy bolts flying out into space. Noting that they seemed to be emanating from the Revocater, Liberty focused on one. The view tracked the bolt, until it hit its target; a seed ship. A number of the arrow-like vessels from the planet were pursuing them.

"Apologies, Liberty Devan entity," Morphus said, again startling Liberty. "I am finding it a challenge to control all aspects of this prototype Revocater. It requires considerably more of my resources than I anticipated."

"I think you're doing great," offered Liberty, but then she wondered if this sounded condescending coming from a mere corporeal being. Then she wondered whether Morphus even understood what condescension was, or if it could be offended at all.

"You cannot offend me," replied Morphus, again evidently reading Liberty's thoughts. "Though I am working to understand your human emotions better."

"You could start by trying to understand the notion of privacy," said Liberty, huffily, though this merely seemed to confuse Morphus into silence. The wall to Liberty's front then switched views again, and a circular blue marker appeared.

"That is your course," said Morphus. "That is our first portal transition back to System 5118208."

Liberty took a deep breath and focused on the marker. She could feel the ship turning towards it and accelerating, yet at the same time, she was oblivious to the change in velocity. It was like sticking one's hand out of the window of a moving car, she mused. Your hand can feel the rush of air moving past it, yet the rest of your body remains protected by the windshield and bodywork.

Liberty continued to focus on the marker, and then tentatively released the controls and waited. The ship did not shudder, and stayed on course.

"You make a fine Revocater pilot, Liberty Devan entity," said Morphus. Liberty was sure she could even hear pride in its voice.

"How long until Goliath realizes we're coming?" said Liberty, turning her thoughts to the task ahead. A seed ship then shot out in front of them, towards the blue marker. Morphus briefly froze, and red bolts of energy lashed out after it, but the seed ship evaded them. A few seconds later, Morphus reanimated, and turned its head to Liberty. The luster of its alien skin seemed to have dulled a little, and Liberty worried that the effort of managing so many of the ship's functions was taking a heavy toll.

"If the great ship does not already suspect, then it will know very soon," it said, ominously. "We have no time to lose..."

CHAPTER 3

Tory Bellona set the Orion down on the landing pad at Gale Basin Spaceport, then shut down the engines and reactor. Even without stepping off the ship, it was immediately apparent to Hudson that the place was almost deserted. Normally, the spaceport at the Basin would be alive with shuttles and transports coming and going. Clearly, even those engaged in the seedier, underworld activities on Mars were more concerned about a potential alien invasion than satisfying their urges, Hudson mused.

Hudson unfastened his harness and turned to Tory. "So, any ideas where we should start looking for Cutler and Griff?"

Tory had already unbuckled her harness and pushed herself out of the seat. She was adjusting her gun belt and webbing pouches, as if she was getting ready for a fight. Which, Hudson realized, she was.

"There are a few places he might try to get an off-grid ship, but my bet is he chose Yaeger's lot," said Tory, finally meeting Hudson's eyes. "She's an asshole, but she hates his guts."

Hudson pushed himself out of the second seat and stretched. He'd asked Tory to fly them to Mars, on account of the copious quantity of whiskey he'd consumed in The Winchester on Deimos Station. Thankfully, the nanoliver capsule that Tory had given him after they'd returned to the Orion had finally cleared the fogginess from his head. "If this Yaeger hates his guts then surely she's not likely to help him?" argued Hudson, following Tory into the corridor leading to the living space.

"Cutler doesn't go cap-in-hand to anyone, but to get what he needs, he'll have to humble himself," replied Tory. "His FS-31 is too hot for even the Basin's bent dealers to touch. But Cutler double-crossed Yaeger some years ago, and she'd love nothing more than to get her own back."

Tory opened a locker next to the semi-circular couch and took out the Model 1873 Winchester rifle she'd taken from Roy the barman. Hudson noticed that the weapon now had a sling attached, including an ammo carrier that held ten rounds of ammunition.

"I may have been a bit drunk when you stole that thing..." said Hudson.

"I've only borrowed it, remember?" Tory interrupted, raising an eyebrow.

"Sure... borrowed," said Hudson, with a wry smile, "but I don't remember it having that harness when it was on the wall in The Winchester."

Tory slung the weapon over her shoulder, and it looked so at home there that Hudson had to remind himself it was a new addition. "I fashioned something while you were asleep," she said.

Hudson frowned, "Fashioned out of what?"

Tory shrugged, "Just out of some material I found, lying around" she said, nonchalantly, while heading towards the cargo bay.

Hudson followed, still wearing a frown. He was getting a bad feeling about Tory's latest accessory. "Found where?" he asked, nervously.

They reached the cargo bay and Tory lowered the rear ramp. The over-warm, humid artificial atmosphere of the Gale Basin rushed in. Tory glanced back at Hudson, the corner of her mouth curling up, playfully. "Let's just say your wardrobe is a little less full than it was before." She then stepped down the ramp, the steel of the Winchester rifle shining under the domed city's warm artificial lights.

Hudson shook his head, "I'm glad I kept my leather jacket on then," he said, walking down beside her.

"I did almost drug you and steal it off your back," said Tory, flatly. "But I'm trying to turn over a new leaf, you know?" She then glanced at Hudson's aghast expression, and raised an eyebrow. "That was a joke," she said, appearing to be disappointed that Hudson hadn't seen the funny side.

"I thought you didn't do jokes?" asked Hudson, not sure if Tory was being serious.

"Apparently, I still don't..."

Hudson laughed, "Hey, that one was actually pretty funny."

"I wasn't joking that time," said Tory, fixing Hudson with her penetrating eyes.

"I think you should probably just stick to intimidating and shooting people," Hudson replied, sarcastically.

They were interrupted by one of the dock workers running up to them. "Hey folks, can I get you any extras today?" he said, coming across as bright and in-your-face as his luminous orange overalls. "Some fuel? Maybe a nice hull polish or an engine tune-up? You're the first customer I've seen all day!"

Tory plucked the credit scanner out of his hand and quickly thumbed it to pay the docking charge. She then shoved it back into the dock worker's chest, knocking the man off balance.

"You don't touch this ship," she began, while narrowing her eyes at him and resting a hand on her six-shooter. "You don't breathe on this ship. In fact, you don't even so much as look at this ship, you got that?"

The man's face drained of blood, and he nervously shuffled around on the spot so that he was no longer facing the Orion. "You got it!" the dock worker said, maintaining his cheerfulness, but his voice wavered as he spoke.

Then Tory plucked a one-hundred-dollar hardbuck note out from inside her armored jacket. She waved it under the dock worker's nose, and shoved it into the breast pocket of his overalls.

"But while you're not touching, breathing or looking at this ship, I want you to make sure no-one else does either," she said.

Hudson was both impressed and disturbed at how easily Tory could switch into her more menacing persona.

"And if anyone does, you make sure to let us know when we get back," Tory added.

The dock worker nodded and offered a tepid smile. "You got it, no problem at all!"

Tory patted him on the shoulder, deliberately hard enough to again unbalance him. "Good. Just remember that if I find you've let down your end of the bargain, I'll be taking that note back." Then she paused, seemingly for dramatic effect. "After I shoot you in the kneecaps."

The dock worker glanced at the Winchester rifle and then at the six-shooter in Tory's belt, and again smiled weakly. Tory glared at him a moment longer, then casually strode away.

The dock worker turned to Hudson, seemingly looking for some reassurance that his partner had been joking. However, as Hudson had just experienced, Tory Bellona didn't do jokes.

"I keep telling her to stop shooting the staff at ports and space stations," Hudson said, shrugging and keeping a straight face. "It does make it hard to find good places to land these days."

Then Hudson left the mildly trembling dock worker behind and caught up with Tory. "You were joking about shooting him, right?" he asked, before following her through the border scanner.

"Didn't you just tell me to stick to intimidating and shooting people?" answered Tory, as she stepped onto the main boulevard for the quadrant.

Hudson had to admit Tory was right, but he also hadn't expected her to take him so literally. "I was being facetious," he said, again following behind her. "You don't have to shoot your way out of every situation, you know?"

Tory stopped suddenly, and Hudson almost walked into the back of her. He was about to ask why she'd halted, but then the answer became clear. Standing in the middle of the boulevard, about ten meters ahead of them, were two men and two women. And they were all wearing the distinctive tailored suits favored by the Council's goons.

Tory turned to Hudson and cocked an eyebrow. "You were saying?"

CHAPTER 4

Tory unslung the Winchester rifle from her shoulder and cocked it; the crisp sound of the lever action mechanism seemed to hang in the air. Hudson reached inside his jacket and slowly drew his pistol, expecting the bullets to immediately start flying. However, curiously, none of the Council thugs had yet drawn their weapons.

"No need for violence, we just want to talk," one of the men called out. The few people that were wandering the boulevard seemed to sense the danger, and quickly disappeared into the seedy establishments that lined the street.

"Then talk," Hudson called back to the man, "We're listening."

The group very slowly started moving towards them. Then the man said, "I think we'd all be more comfortable if we spoke somewhere off the boulevard, don't you?" He'd phrased it as a question, but from the tone of his voice, Hudson could tell he didn't care what they thought.

Tory glanced over her shoulder, and then peered up at the higher levels of the buildings around them. "Four more behind us, and at least two spotting on the upper levels," she said, keeping her voice low.

Hudson didn't look back, but he quickly scanned the windows and balconies ahead, and saw at least one of the people Tory had mentioned. "I think the odds are a little against us in a shoot-out," he said, also keeping his voice low. "Is there another way off this boulevard?"

Tory glanced to her right, "We can cut through that massage parlor and onto the service alley out the back," she said, as Hudson surreptitiously glanced to where she'd indicated. "It's close to one of the ground transitways. If we're lucky, we might be able to hijack a transport. If not, we can slip into the lower level; they'll be less willing to follow us there."

Hudson had heard enough stories about the Basin's lower level to know it was the last place – besides where he was now – that he wanted to be. However, he wasn't enamored about venturing inside the massage parlor either. From the look of the place, it seemed to be offering a very different type of service.

"How do you know where this massage parlor leads to?" Hudson asked. Then he realized he'd perhaps come off sounding a little confrontational.

Tory turned to him, "Really? You're choosing right now to ask me that?"

Hudson didn't answer; his attention was again drawn to the group of four Council goons, who were still creeping closer. A couple of them had pulled back their jackets to reveal their weapons. He glanced behind and saw the second group was closing in too. Despite his misgivings, he had to accept that a seedy massage parlor was preferable to getting gunned down on the boulevard.

"Okay, you lead – since you obviously know the way..." Tory rolled her eyes at him, "and I'll follow."

Tory immediately ran, firing shots from the hip with the Winchester. The bullets pinged off the road surface at the feet of the goons, causing them to scatter for cover. Hudson was glad of the clear head that Tory's nanoliver had given him, and he reacted swiftly, chasing after Tory, while firing blindly into the air. Tory smashed through the screen door of the parlor, and Hudson practically fell in behind her, as gunshots rang out in from the boulevard.

"No, Werner wants them alive!" Hudson heard a voice call out, as he charged further into the establishment. Semi-naked men and women scattered like ninepins, as Tory bustled past them and into a back room. Hudson regained his balance and chased after her, pushing through into the next space. He didn't consider himself bashful, but even he had to force himself to look ahead, to avoid witnessing the fleshy scenes all around him.

"Hurry, we're almost there!" Tory called back, as she launched her boot at a door, smashing it open.

Hudson glanced behind, seeing that the Council thugs were in pursuit, but then he discovered Tory locked in a struggle with another suited goon. There was a stairwell close to the door, and Hudson assumed the man had just charged down from the upper level.

The thug had grabbed Tory's rifle and was trying to wrestle her to her knees. Hudson darted forward and clubbed the goon's fingers with his pistol, crushing them against the stock of the Winchester. The man cried out and released his hold, allowing Tory to throw him to one side, before hammering the butt of the rifle into his head.

Hudson and Tory exchanged a brief glance, and then Tory ran ahead. Hudson turned, firing two more shots into the air. Plaster crumbled down from the ceiling, and again the Council goons were forced to scatter and temporarily abort their pursuit. Hudson pushed on harder and caught up with Tory, as she leveled her boot at a sturdier-looking metal door. This time it didn't budge.

"Give me a hand!" Tory shouted, stepping back and readying herself for another charge. Hudson ran to her side, and then nodded, before they both launched perfectly timed kicks together. The door flew open into the service alley, and they both bundled through it, but waiting outside were three more suited goons.

Tory didn't pause even for a nanosecond, taking advantage of their surprise arrival to attack first. She clubbed the nearest man with the Winchester, knocking him out cold, while Hudson tackled the second, driving him into the side of a commercial-sized waste container. He saw Tory take a hit to the head and body, but she parried the next blow and launched a ferocious counter-attack. Driving the butt of the Winchester solidly into the man's gut, she then spun a kick to his head, before slamming him into the side wall. Hudson heard the organic snap as his head split open, like a coconut being cracked with a hammer.

The thug pulled Hudson up and punched him twice to the head and body, but he was no stranger to street brawls either. Blocking the next strike, he then landed a low blow, before driving his knee into the nose of the man, as he bent double. The crunch of bone and cartilage was unmistakable.

Hudson quickly turned back to the rear door of the parlor, and saw another waste container just to its side. "Help me move this!" he called over to Tory, while running over to the container.

Together, they hauled the heavy object in front of the door, a split-second before fists began to hammer against it and angry voices filled the air.

Tory slapped Hudson on the back, "Let's move!" she cried, before charging off towards the transitway.

Winded and gasping for breath, Hudson followed as quickly as he could, but he couldn't quite keep pace with Tory. "Are you sure you're not a damn robot, like Morphus?", wheezed Hudson, wondering where she got her strength and stamina from.

"I've just had more practice escaping from Council goons than you have," Tory called back, as she slid to a stop at the edge of the side road.

The transitway, like the spaceport, was oddly deserted, but Hudson spotted a large, black ground transit parked about ten meters away.

"There, we can take that!" he called to Tory, pointing over to the vehicle. Then he ran, but Tory suddenly shouted out to him.

"No, Hudson wait!"

Hudson slid to a stop, meters from the transit, then the side door slid open. Four suited Council goons piled out, each carrying sub-machine guns. There was a crash from behind and Hudson glanced back, seeing that the waste container had been pushed from the door. The other eight Council thugs were now coming through. He met Tory's eyes, and he could see the anger and hatred for the Council swelling inside her. She gripped the Winchester and chambered another round.

"Tory, don't!" Hudson called out, realizing she was planning on going out shooting. "We can talk this out. We can explain!"

Tory raised the Winchester, but then a voice spoke up and she instantly froze.

"Listen to the smart man, Tory Bellona," said the soothing voice, before Werner stepped out of the transit. "Then he looked at Hudson, and smiled his kindly-uncle smile. "Hudson Powell, I presume? I've heard so much about you. I'm glad we can finally meet."

Hudson frowned, and quickly glanced back at Tory. Six of the eight suited Council thugs were aiming their pistols at her, but she now had the Winchester aimed at Werner's head.

"Who are you?" he asked the older man, "and how do you know my name?"

The Council boss smiled. "My name is Werner Nest. Your friend Tory knows me well." Then he looked up at Tory, and smiled an even more insincere smile. "Isn't that right, Tory?"

"What do you want Werner?" said Tory, bitterly.

"To talk, that's all," Werner replied, opening his palms towards them. "There is much we need to discuss."

"I've no interest in talking to you," spat Tory. "So, either get out of our way, or get a bullet from this rifle."

Werner sighed, "Stubborn, to the last," he said, wistfully. Then he blinked his eyes towards one of the suited men behind Tory, and before Hudson could even utter a scream, the thug had squeezed his trigger, and fired.

CHAPTER 5

The hood was whipped off Hudson's head, forcing him to squint against the sudden influx of light. His eyes began to adjust, and he saw that he was in some sort of warehouse or industrial unit. There were a dozen or so shipping containers inside, some of which appeared to function as makeshift offices or meeting spaces. Werner was standing behind a clinical-looking metal table a short distance away, with two suited Council thugs behind him. Both held compact semi-automatic weapons and wore threatening expressions to match their lethal armaments.

Hudson heard the bootsteps of someone approaching him from behind. Then the binders that were put on his hands in the service alley, along with the hood, were removed, and a suited thug appeared just behind and to his side. Hudson recognized him as the heavy-set man who had shot Tory.

The goons had rushed Hudson and pulled the hood over his head, before he could see whether Tory was alive or dead. They'd then bundled him into the transit, but not before dealing a few hard kicks and punches for good measure. However, even though Hudson hadn't been able to judge Tory's condition, he knew that the man had shot her in the body. Because of this, there was a good chance that Tory's armored jacket would have saved her. That hope was all that was preventing him from losing his cool, or breaking down completely. Hudson wasn't sure which would come first.

With his eyes fully-adjusted to the light, Hudson looked around the new space. Other than Werner and the three Council goons, there appeared to be no-one else there.

"Please, come closer, Mr. Powell," said Werner, warmly beckoning Hudson to approach with a gentle wave of his hand. Hudson then noticed that his pistol, plus Tory's six-shooter and Winchester rifle were laid out on the table.

"Where's Tory?" asked Hudson, standing his ground. He stood tall and sounded assured, but was careful not to appear rude or disrespectful. "Is she okay?"

The thug to his side shoved him in the back, causing Hudson to stumble two steps closer to the table. He glowered back at the man, but the thug just smiled sadistically, almost willing Hudson to make a move. However, from his own experience of the Council on New Providence, plus what Liberty had told him, Hudson knew better than to provoke them.

"Fear not, Tory Bellona is still alive," said Werner, smoothly, before adding, "for now." The last two words were delivered with a threatening dash of menace. "Whether she remains that way very much depends on you, Mr. Powell."

"Where is she?" asked Hudson, again fighting hard to keep from lashing out. "Is she here?"

"She is being interviewed about what happened on New Providence," Werner replied, though his eyes were sharpening a touch. Hudson could tell that his constant questions were already irritating the Council boss. "Once this interview has been completed, you shall be reunited."

Hudson huffed a laugh. He could well imagine what kind of interview they were conducting. "Are you asking about when Liberty escaped from your prison?" said Hudson, starting to feel the grip on his emotions slipping. Werner's eyes narrowed a touch. "Tory had nothing to do with that. Liberty was just more accomplished than you gave her credit for." He wasn't sure whether lying was a good idea, but he had to do what he could to help Tory.

"Yet here Tory is, with you, Liberty Devan's relic-hunter partner," replied Werner, and Hudson cursed himself silently for walking himself into an obvious corner. "This seems to me to be more than a coincidence, no?"

Hudson fought to contain the swell of uneasiness he now felt, and thought on his feet. "Since you seem to know so much, you probably also know that Tory was originally hired to kill me," he said, trying to throw doubt on Werner's suspicions. "Logan Griff and Cutler Wendell double-crossed her, and I picked up her services instead," he continued, before shrugging. "She's a hired gun, and that's all there is to it."

Werner leant forward on the table and peered into Hudson's eyes. "I doubt that very much," he replied, though this time there was no trace of his earlier, affable demeanor. Werner's eyes had hardened, and his entire body language had also changed, as if Hudson had just issued a challenge. "Liberty Devan was sold to me in a fair bargain," Werner continued with the same composed malevolence. "The ill-mannered RGF officer and Cutler Wendell owe me compensation for her escape. But I will settle for reclaiming my debts with Tory, if I have to."

Hudson frowned back at him, "What the hell does that mean?"

Werner rose up and pressed his hands behind his back. "It means that I will take Tory back into my indentured service as payment."

"You can't, she'll die before going back to the Council!" Hudson hit back.

Werner merely returned an oily smile; seeming to delight in having finally cracked Hudson's thin veneer of composure. "There is an alternative," said Werner, in a smooth manner that made Hudson think he'd planned this all along. "We are aware of the alien crystal that has the ability to locate and open new portals." Hudson forced down a dry swallow, realizing what Werner was going to ask for. "I know that Cutler traded it somewhere inside this city," Werner continued. "I assume that is why you are here."

Shit, Cutler has already traded the crystal? thought Hudson, surprised that they would let it go. He tried to keep his expression blank, so as not to give anything away to Werner, but the return of the Council boss's repellant sneer told him that he'd already read between the lines.

"Tell me who has the crystal, and how to use it, Mr. Powell, and I will consider all debts paid in full," Werner finished.

Hudson shook his head, "You don't understand; that crystal is the only thing that can stop the alien vessel that's destroying the portal worlds," he said, pleading with Werner, but the Council boss appeared utterly unconcerned. Hudson couldn't believe what he was seeing and hearing; even faced with the threat of annihilation, this poisonous snake was still thinking of personal profit. "Your own space station was destroyed!" he continued, anger seeping into his voice. "Six planets have already crumbled to dust. Millions are dead!"

Werner slammed a fist on the table, causing the weapons on its surface to bounce. "I do not care about these planets!" he roared. "And Earth can burn too for all I care – I want that crystal!"

The sudden ferocity of Werner's reaction stunned Hudson into silence. He hadn't realized how unhinged Werner was until that moment, and it only made him more dangerous. Hudson remained silent as Werner then forced his eyes shut, and took several deep breaths. When he spoke again, it was with more composure.

"The Martian and Earth fleets will deal with this alien invader you speak of," Werner continued, dismissing the threat as if it were a simple case of trespassing. "Then, once the dust has quite literally settled, the system of portal worlds will need to be rebuilt. And with that crystal, I will hold the key to all the new gateways. I will control it all."

Hudson laughed, which caused Werner's jaw to visibly tighten. "If I don't get that crystal back, there will be no-one left alive to rebuild," he said. Exasperation had replaced anger; he knew there was no reasoning with people like these. "Goliath will kill us all. Humanity will be wiped out."

Werner held Hudson's eyes for a few seconds, then sighed, "I had hoped we could reach an accord, like two reasonable men, but I see now that you are as stubborn and blinkered as your new companion." Werner then turned to one of the men behind him, "Bring her..."

Hudson waited nervously as the suited thug walked across the warehouse floor and went into one of the shipping containers. A few seconds later, he returned with another suited guard, who was pushing Tory in front of him at the barrel of his sub-machine gun. Hudson could see that she had blood around her nose and mouth, and matted blood in her long, dark hair. Her hands were bound in front of her.

Anger swelled inside Hudson, and he tried to go to Tory, but the armed thug behind him grabbed Hudson's shoulder, and pressed his weapon into his kidneys. "This is madness, killing us won't get you what you want!" Hudson shouted, still struggling against the strength of guard holding him. Then Hudson was struck to the side of the head, and the force and suddenness of the blow rocked him to his knees. Tory met his eyes, but her expression was as cold and hard as steel.

"Killing both of you?" replied Werner coolly. "No, Mr. Powell, that won't get me what I want." Then he picked up Hudson's pistol from the table, and walked to Tory's side, careful not to get too close. Werner casually raised the pistol, and aimed it at Tory's head. "But I suspect that threatening to kill your new partner here might motivate you."

Hudson felt panic rising in his gut, but Tory still did not react. "If you kill her, then why would I help you?" he said, again trying to think on his feet, but their situation seemed hopeless.

"Because, if I must, Mr. Powell, I will torture you for information about the crystal," Werner replied, matter-of-factly. "I admit, the prospect bores me. But rest assured, I will get what I want, one way or another. The only difference is how many lives are lost, and how much blood is shed." Werner then straightened his arm, and slipped his finger onto the trigger. "I suggest you choose now."

"Okay, I'll tell you, just don't shoot!" Hudson called out, and again, he received an oily smile in return. Hudson glanced to Tory, expecting her to tell him to keep quiet, but she made no sound. She merely looked back at Werner with the same, unyielding eyes. Unopposed, Hudson turned back to Werner, and continued, "The truth is that I didn't know Cutler had already traded the crystal till you told me. But if he has, then it's likely that it was to someone called Yaeger. She owns one of the shipyard lots here in the Basin."

"An intelligent choice," said Werner, lowering the pistol. "However, Tory will remain my guest, until we've verified your information."

Suddenly, Hudson heard a series of low beeps coming from somewhere nearby. The sound was faint, and hard to pinpoint, but everyone, Werner included, began looking around trying to find the source.

"What is that sound?" snapped Werner, angrily turning to the guard behind Tory.

"It's a skelly," said Tory, breaking her self-imposed silence. Her voice was composed, but her eyes burned with rage.

Werner frowned, and then looked down at her binders. "You fools didn't search her?" he yelled.

However, Tory didn't give any of the suited goons a chance to answer. The beeps stopped and the binders fell away, but even before they had hit the ground, Tory had grabbed the arm of the thug behind her and flung him into Werner. The Council boss was propelled backwards, bowling over one of the other guards. The third raised his weapon and fired, but Tory was already charging at him. Hudson figured he must have hit her, but the combination of Tory's armored jacket, plus her momentum, carried her through him like a freight train.

The guard behind Hudson shoved him aside, and raised his sub-machine gun at Tory, but adrenalin was now surging through Hudson's veins. He darted back, barging into the man and upsetting his aim. The weapon fired a short burst, but the rounds flew wide.

Wasting no time, Hudson grasped the guard's sub-machine gun, and tore it from his grasp. He took a solid right to the face, but shook it off, and drove the butt of the weapon into the guard's gut. The goon absorbed the blow, and managed to grab hold of Hudson's jacket, wrestling him to the ground. The guard was stronger and carried another fifty pounds on Hudson, but he managed to slip out of the hold and get behind him. He then pulled the sub-machine gun up against the guard's throat, trying to choke the air and strength from the thick-set thug. The man fought for his life, trying desperately to force the weapon away, while writhing in an attempt to free himself. However, Hudson held on, muscles burning, and battling with all the strength left in him.

Werner and the other three goons were still down, but Tory was already back to her feet. And though she had initially gained the upper hand, even Hudson doubted she could prevail in a four-on-one gunfight. Hudson could only watch as Tory rushed back to the metal table, turned it over, and dove over the top of it. Werner scrambled to his feet and fled, as the guards recovered their weapons and took aim. They then rained bullets into the table, pock-marking the thick metal like dimpled deck plating, but the shield had served its purpose and Tory was unhurt.

Hudson tried to call out to her, but all of his energy was consumed with trying to win the struggle with the guard. Even if he had managed to raise his voice, Tory would not have heard him. Her expression was wrought into a look of brutal determination, fueled by fury and years of resentment and hatred towards the Council. Hudson was unable to help or intervene as Tory snatched up the Winchester rifle that had slid on to the floor nearby. To Hudson's horror, Tory then stood up, directly in the line of fire. The guards initially stopped shooting, clearly baffled as to why Tory had shown herself, but then a fraction of second later, Tory began shooting. She had aimed and reloaded the famous lever-action rifle with frightening efficiency, shooting all three suited thugs cleanly in the head in a matter of seconds. Tory then turned the weapon towards Werner and fired again, but the Council boss had already slipped behind a shipping container, and the bullet just thudded harmlessly into the metal. Tory roared in frustration and ran after him, but then she saw Hudson, still struggling with the guard, and stopped in her tracks.

The momentary distraction allowed the suited thug to break free, and reverse the hold. He felt the man's immense bulk press down on him, and the metal crush his throat. Then there was another crack of rifle fire, and the pressure on his throat disappeared. Pushing the goon off him, he saw Tory approaching, smoke seeping from the barrel of the Winchester.

"Thanks..." croaked Hudson, rubbing his aching neck. Then he saw blood trickling down Tory's side. The material of the armored jacket had split. "Hey, you're shot!" he said, scrambling to his knees.

"It's fine, the jacket kept it out," she said, in a 'don't fuss' kind of voice. "Just another cut for me to stitch up, and a broken rib or two. I'll be fine."

Hudson could see that she appeared more in control of her emotions now, but her eyes were still cold and severe. "Are you okay?" he asked, but then quickly clarified his question, "And I don't mean the cut and cracked ribs. I mean you."

Tory glared in the direction that Werner had run. "I will be when I find that rat bastard," she snarled, before offering a hand to Hudson. He took it, and Tory helped him to his feet.

"Werner will have to wait," Hudson said, finally managing to talk without sounding like a fifty-a-day smoker. "Werner knows about Yaeger now. So, if she does have the crystal then we have to get to her first. We don't have much time."

For a moment, it looked like Tory was about to argue back, but then she gave Hudson a resigned nod instead. She collected her six-shooter off the floor, placing it back in her holster, then picked up Hudson's pistol. She turned back and offered it to him.

"These work better when you actually shoot people with them, rather than try to choke them out," she said, cocking an eyebrow at him.

Hudson huffed a laugh, "True, but I think there's already been enough shooting for one day."

Then Tory's eyes became severe again. "I doubt these will be the last shots fired, before we leave the Gale Basin." She opened Hudson's jacket, and slotted the weapon into his shoulder holster. "Come on, let's find that crystal so we can get off this dump."

CHAPTER 6

The warehouse that Hudson and Tory had been abducted to by Werner and his goons was in an industrial sector of the basin. Ordinarily, it would have been teeming with freight and logistics traffic, but the looming threat of Goliath had caused many of the businesses to shut up or scale down. As such, it had been the perfect location for a spot of quiet torture and murder, Hudson realized. Once again, he'd walked the tightrope between life and death, and once again it had been Tory Bellona's proficiency for violence that had saved his neck.

Fortunately, Werner's black transit had still been parked outside the warehouse unit, and thanks to a further employment of Tory's skelly, Hudson had managed to break in and hack the ignition system. There was still some ground traffic moving on the transitways – enough for their journey to section thirteen to not appear too conspicuous. However, as they approached the perimeter gate into the Basin's shipyard district, Hudson suddenly noticed the ID scanners on the towers.

"Whoa, hold up," Hudson said to Tory, who was driving. He pointed up at the gate, "There are scanners on the perimeter; if we pass through here, we'll get identified, and Werner will know where we are."

Tory glanced up at the scanners, but continued driving the transit towards the perimeter. "Werner knows where we're headed, anyway," she said, glancing at Hudson. "We should assume he's already heading here too, with another gang of goons."

Hudson shrugged and nodded, though he didn't relish the prospect of another run in with armed Council thugs, "Fair point. At least we've got a head start on him." Then he had a thought, "What if there are ID scanners inside too?" he asked. "Given our turbulent history with Admiral Shelby, I wouldn't put it past her to send a squad of MP security after us."

Tory shook her head, "I doubt that will happen. The MP largely keep their noses out of the business that goes on in here," she replied. "It's all part of the deal the MP did with the Council. They keep the riff-raff contained in the Basin, and the MP turns a blind eye to some of the Council's less above-board business ventures."

Hudson laughed, "And here's me thinking all Martians were strait-laced, uptight assholes."

"People are people, wherever you go," said Tory, with a sort of cold indifference and harsh worldliness. "In my experience, most people are assholes."

Hudson raised an eyebrow. "This is the part where you're supposed to say, 'present company excepted'."

"If I thought you were an asshole, I'd have shot you in the alien hulk on Vivaldi One," said Tory. Her mood was still brittle, and Hudson's attempts at levity hadn't had a softening effect. He realized then that her encounter with Werner and the Council must have had a deeper impact than he'd first thought.

Tory drove the transit through the perimeter gate, and headed straight into the shipyard district. Unlike the rest of the Gale Basin that they'd seen, the shipyard district still appeared to be fairly busy.

"Dump the transit on the side of the road, here," said Hudson, pointing to an area up ahead. "We should walk the rest of the way."

Tory scowled at him, "Why, when we have a transit? Besides, I hate walking."

"If the scanners did identify us on the way in, then leaving the transit here might make Werner's goons take a detour to check it out," Hudson replied. "It might only delay them by a minute or two, but I'll take any advantage we can get."

"Okay, but did I mention I hate walking?" Tory grumbled, before pulling the transit over and switching off its motor. She then grabbed the Winchester rifle from the rear seat, and loaded more rounds into it from the ammo loop on the strap. "Be ready for another fight," said Tory, cheerlessly, while grabbing the door handle.

"Hopefully, we'll be in and out before the Council arrive," replied Hudson, but Tory shook her head.

"I meant with Yaeger," said Tory. "She's a tough old bird."

Hudson sighed and nodded again; the Gale Basin was quickly topping the list of places in the galaxy where he least wanted to be. He then opened his door and stepped outside, remaining vigilant for any sign of suited Council heavies. Tory led the way onto the massive central expanse that contained the dozens of shipyard lots. It was then that Hudson noticed many of the dealers were in the process of shutting up shop, and moving their ships into the cavernous hangar areas to the sides. Nevertheless, there was a roaring trade going on, as dealers appeared to be heavily discounting their stock in order to shift as many ships as possible.

"If this bunch of sharks are getting twitchy then the news about Goliath must be getting worse," said Tory, who appeared to have observed the same unusual behavior.

"Maybe you can buy back Cutler's FS-31," said Hudson, smiling. He was still attempting to crack Tory's wall of ice. "I'm sure that would get his back up."

There was still not even the faintest flicker of a smile from Tory. "If I bought that ship, the first thing I'd do is torch it," she said, acidly. "That might make me feel a bit better." Then she pointed to a lot about a hundred meters ahead. "There, that one is Yaeger's shipyard."

Hudson looked over and saw a few customers milling around the various ships on the lot. They were being carefully watched by a middle-aged woman in what looked like well-worn relic-hunter gear. Hudson had spent enough time in bars and diners in the less salubrious ports in the galaxy to recognize someone who could handle themselves. And despite what Yaeger was now, Hudson knew that at one time she had been a fighter.

Yaeger appeared to spot Tory and Hudson as they entered the lot, and started to walk towards them. Hudson quickly realized that there wasn't an FS-31 Patrol Craft on any of the stands. Either Cutler had traded his ship to someone else, or Yaeger had already sold it. And if that was the case, he worried that the dealer may have already moved the crystal too.

"Well, well, well, if it isn't Cutler Wendell's ball-breaking former partner," said Yaeger, stopping in front of them and folding her arms. She then scanned Hudson from head to toe. "At least your new partner is a little easier on the eye, I'll give you that," she said, winking at Hudson. "I hope he's less of an asshole than Cutler Wendell too."

Hudson stepped forward and offered his hand to Yaeger, "Honestly, that's not difficult," he said, smiling at the rugged-looking dealer. "I'm Hudson, by the way."

"I only shake hands when a deal is done, Hudson 'by the way'," Yaeger replied. Though Hudson's charm had seemed to soften her up a little.

"Cutler is why we're here," said Tory, who had also folded her arms, and was noticeably less friendly than Hudson had been. "I take it that since you know we're no longer partners, that you've seen him recently?"

Hudson was impressed at Tory's intuition. And judging from the scowl on Yaeger's face, she appeared annoyed that she'd inadvertently given that information away.

"Yeah, that piece of shit was here," said Yaeger, matching Tory's standoffishness. "What of it?"

"Did he trade you a crystal?" said Hudson, deciding to step in, before the two women progressed to arm wrestling, or some other contest to show who was toughest. "If so, it's vital we get it back."

Yaeger now scowled at Hudson. "Get it back? So, Cutler stole it from you, did he?" she said, before tutting. "Figures."

"It was actually another first-class asshole named Logan Griff that stole it," Hudson corrected her. "But yes, it was stolen from us. And if we don't get it back, a lot of people are going to die."

Yaeger's eyes flicked over to Tory, who was still standing statuesque, like a nightclub bouncer. "Why?" she then said, looking back at Hudson, "What's so important about that crystal?"

"It would take too long to explain fully," replied Hudson, "But assuming you've read the epapers recently, you must know about the alien ship that's been destroying the outer portal world planets?"

Yaeger laughed, as if Hudson's question was the dumbest she'd ever heard. "Well, duh. That's why everyone here is bugging out, and going crazy with flash sales. It's wrecking my trade."

"That crystal is the only thing that can stop it," Hudson continued, "I realize you don't know me from the next random guy who enters your lot, but I need you to trust me."

Yaeger held Hudson's eyes for a moment, and then burst out laughing. "You must think I'm some kind of mug," she said, wiping a tear from her eye. "But, full marks for effort." Hudson tried to protest and convince Yaeger that he was telling the truth, but the dealer was having none of it. "Look, Hudson 'by the way', if you want that crystal, you're going to have to come up with some serious credits," Yaeger continued. "I'm talking a minimum of seven zeros." Then she plucked a set of ID fobs from her belt and jangled them in front of Hudson. "Otherwise, that crystal stays safely locked up." Then Yaeger glanced at Tory, who was eyeing the set of keyfobs. "And don't even think about trying to take these. My lock-up is booby-trapped to hell." She folded her arms again, and stared at Tory. "You ain't the only one who was a relic hunter, lady."

Hudson tried to think of another approach that might reach Yaeger, but Tory was clearly done talking. She cocked the Winchester rifle and aimed it at the dealer's chest. Yaeger stepped back, and seemed genuinely threatened. Despite her bluster, and her own tough talking, she clearly knew that Tory's reputation had been well-earned.

"I've not met a booby trap I can't defeat yet," said Tory, "So give me that set of fobs, or I'll blow a hole in your chest and take them."

"Tory, wait..." said Hudson, recognizing the glacially cold look in her eyes.

"Look, do you want to stop Goliath or not?" Tory snapped, cutting Hudson off. "Because billions will die if we don't get that crystal soon." Then she nodded dismissively towards Yaeger. "What's one low-life ship dealer compared to that?"

Yaeger looked at Hudson, then back at Tory. There was fear behind her eyes, but she was desperately trying to hide it. "You're bluffing," Yaeger hit back at Tory, but Hudson could hear the uncertainty in her voice. "You won't shoot me in plain sight. The MP will arrest you before you even get out of this sector."

Tory slipped her finger onto the trigger. "I'll do what I have to."

Suddenly, there were frightened shouts from outside the lot, and Hudson looked out to see a large ground transport driving towards them. He recognized it as the same style of black transit that Werner had used, and quickly pushed the barrel of the Winchester away from Yaeger's chest.

"It's the Council," he said, as Tory glowered at him, "They've found us, we need to go."

"Werner Nest?" said Yaeger, rapidly backing away, "The Council boss? What the hell are you two crooks into?"

Tory spun around and aimed at the transport, before firing three rounds in rapid succession, each smashing through the vehicle's windshield. There were more screams and yells, as people fled for cover. Then the transport screeched to a halt just outside the lot, and the side door flew open.

"Get that set of ID fobs!" Tory shouted over to Hudson. She grabbed his leather jacket and pulled him closer, "Whatever it takes, you have to get those fobs." Hudson had never seen her so focused and intense. "I'll hold them off. Now go!"

Hudson pulled out his pistol and ran after Yaeger, firing back at the black transit, as four Council guards darted out and took cover behind the vehicle. Yaeger was already sprinting towards her office cabin with remarkable pace, but Hudson was still gaining on her. Then the buzz of semi-automatic weapons filled the air, and Hudson heard the rounds pinging off the hulls of nearby shuttles. Yaeger was hit in the calf, and she yelped in pain and almost fell, but managed to hobble on towards the building. Hudson turned and took another shot at the ground transport, but then he heard the distinctive sound of the Winchester firing again and again. He saw that Tory had taken cover behind the undercarriage of a nearby freighter. Two guards were already on the ground; victims both of the powerful antique weapon, and of Tory's expert aim.

Hudson had almost caught up with Yaeger just as she barged open the door to her office. He raced in after her, but was then met with the barrel of a shotgun.

"Stop right there, or I blow your head off!" Yaeger yelled at him. Her face was contorted in pain, and blood was leaking onto the floor from the wound to her leg.

"I have to get that crystal back," Hudson said again, still hoping that reason would prevail. "Give me the fob, and we'll be out of your hair. You won't get an offer like that from Werner."

Yaeger's eyes narrowed, "He's after that thing too?" Hudson nodded. "Damn it, I knew that asshole Wendell and his clobber friend gave it up too easily," she yelled. Then she jabbed the weapon towards Hudson, as the sound of gunfire continued to echo outside. "Just tell me one thing straight," she said, sounding suddenly more serious. "This cockamamy story about the crystal being the only thing that can stop that rampaging alien ship. That's just bullshit, right?"

Hudson shook his head, "I wish it was, believe me I do. But without that crystal, no planet is safe, not even Earth."

There was a tense silence, before Yaeger yelled, "Shit!" almost at the top of her voice. Hudson nearly jumped out of his skin. Then to his surprise, Yaeger lowered the shotgun, before reaching down and unclipping the set of ID fobs from her belt. "Garage twenty-seven, east side," she said, removing one of the fobs and throwing it at him. She then slumped down into her office chair, groaning as she stretched her bleeding leg out in front of her. "The crystal is in my desk drawer, inside a cigar box."

Hudson caught the square plastic fob and closed his fist around it. "Thank you," he said, with such deep sincerity that Yaeger seemed genuinely taken aback; but then the dealer scowled and waved him off.

"Just get the hell out of here," she snarled, "and take that lunatic mercenary with you, before she shoots holes in the rest of my stock."

Hudson noticed that the firing had stopped. He peered outside, and saw Tory backing towards the office. Four suited Council thugs lay dead on the tarmac by the ground transit.

"You've done the right thing," said Hudson, turning back to Yaeger. "If we all survive this, I'll pay you back somehow." This again seemed to catch Yaeger off guard, and she just looked at him, as if he were an alien.

Hudson stepped out of the door, but then Yaeger called out to him. "Hey, Hudson 'by the way'," she said, her tone now almost genial. "The office is by the stairwell, and I wasn't kidding about the booby traps, so watch your step." Then she pointed to her leg, "I'd help you, but I got problems of my own."

Hudson nodded, "I will, thanks again."

Tory appeared at the door, saw the ID fob in Hudson's hand, and looked at Yaeger's bleeding leg.

"Did you shoot her?" Tory asked, peering at Hudson with a curious frown.

"No, of course not!" replied Hudson, genuinely affronted at the accusation.

Tory made a sort of disappointed huffing sound, and said, "That's a shame. For a moment, I was almost impressed." Then she turned around and left.

CHAPTER 7

Unsurprisingly, the open-air gunfight with the Council thugs had quickly gotten the attention of the MP security forces. However, Hudson and Tory had succeeded in making a swift getaway, before the forces had shown up. They were now roaming the perimeter of the shipyard district, heading towards Yaeger's lock-up. No-one had paid them any attention, or seemed to recognize them as participants in the firefight. One advantage to the sector being relatively deserted was that there were few witnesses. And, if Hudson had judged the prickly and standoffish character of Yaeger correctly, she was not the sort to willingly co-operate with the authorities. He was confident that Yaeger would not reveal anything to the security forces about him, Tory or the crystal.

They soon reached garage twenty-seven and Hudson fished the ID fob out of his jacket pocket.

He was about to hold it against the lock of the side door, but Tory grabbed his hand and stopped him.

"Hold up," she said, frowning at the door. "Remember that Yaeger warned us about this place being booby trapped."

Hudson nodded and quickly withdrew his hand. "You know Yaeger; what would she do?" he asked, hoping that Tory's greater experience would yield some insight.

Tory shrugged, "I don't know her that well," she admitted, "but she's a cunning old fox, so I'd expect the traps to be well laid." Tory examined the door more closely, but then shrugged again. "I guess we just take it slow, and hope that Yaeger hasn't rigged up anything too nasty."

Hudson laughed, "No guts, no glory, right?"

Tory took the ID fob from his hand, and pressed it to the lock. "Hopefully, at least no guts," she said, with the faintest hint of a smile.

"Didn't we agree that you'd avoid telling jokes, and just stick to intimidating and shooting people?" Hudson replied, as the lock clicked open.

"Who's joking?" replied Tory, darkly, before she pushed the door ever so slightly ajar. With the attentiveness of an archeologist, she then surveyed the frame, looking for any indication that Yaeger had set a trap. A few seconds later, Tory smiled and met Hudson's eyes. "Round one to us," she said, reaching up and clicking a button, before pushing the door open fully.

Hudson moved closer and saw a switch built into the door frame on the inside. He nodded in appreciation of Tory's eagle-eyed spot. "Good catch," he said, before stepping inside.

"Boom!" yelled Tory, and Hudson nearly jumped out of his skin for the second time that hour.

"Shit, Tory, that wasn't funny!" Hudson snarled, trying to keep his voice low.

But Tory just shrugged, strolled in beside Hudson and closed the door behind them. "Yeah, yeah, stick to intimidating and shooting people, I get it."

Hudson shook his head, finally managing to see the funny side. "Yaeger said the crystal was in her desk drawer, by the stairwell," he said. He quickly surveyed the garage space and saw a steep metal stairway leading up to a high mezzanine level, but there was no sign of a desk near it. "My guess is that her office must be up on that mezzanine," he said, pointing towards the top of the staircase. Tory didn't answer, and was instead seemingly staring off into space.

"Hey, Tory, are you still with me?" asked Hudson, before following the line of her gaze. Then he saw what had captured Tory's attention; it was Cutler Wendell's FS-31 Patrol Craft. Hudson turned back to Tory, guessing at what she was probably thinking. "Hey, keep your head in the game. We're here for the crystal, nothing else."

Tory met his eyes, then her stony expression softened slightly. "I know, you're right," she said, before casting her intense eyes back at the FS-31. "But I'd still love to take a sledgehammer to that damn ship." Then she again turned to Hudson, and added, "Come on, and watch your step. The device in the door won't be the only trap in this garage."

Tory led them across the garage, creeping as carefully as a cat burglar, with Hudson matching her step for step. They eventually reached the foot of the metal stairwell, without being blown up, caught in a net, or otherwise snared or maimed, before Tory indicated for Hudson to stop.

"It looks like she also uses this mezzanine level as some kind of living space," said Tory, pointing to a couch against the railings. "If that's the case, she'll have definitely protected the route up. So, let me check it out first."

"Okay, but be careful," Hudson replied, "you might be tough, but you're not invulnerable."

"Don't worry, I've survived worse than Yaeger," replied Tory, but it wasn't spoken as a boast, and so offered Hudson some reassurance.

Tory began to slowly ascend the stairs, one step at a time. Each time, she checked the next step up, scouting for pressure plates or other sensors. Her progress was slow and laborious, and Hudson found his attention wandering to other items in the garage. Then, on the wall underneath the stairs, Hudson saw what looked like scrape marks. He checked again on Tory's progress, but she still had about a fifth of the stairway to traverse, so he decided to check it out.

Running his hand along the groove, it felt like they had been gouged out by something sharp and heavy. The marks also progressed in a shallow arc, as if they had been made using a giant protractor. Hudson scowled, unable to piece it all together, but then he looked up at the underside of the stairwell, and saw a sturdy metal hinge. His heart began to race as he checked underneath the stairwell next to it and saw that there was a clean break. The stairwell was split in two distinct sections, and Hudson instantly guessed the terrible reason why.

"Shit! Tory, don't move any further!" Hudson called out, realizing what had carved out the grooves. Yaeger had rigged the stairway to collapse. "The stairs themselves are the trap!" he shouted.

It was too late. There was a sharp click as Tory triggered the mechanism and the entire upper half of the heavy metal staircase swung down directly towards Hudson. He dove out of the way at the last second, narrowly avoiding being smashed in the face, but then he saw Tory, dangling by one hand from the floor of the mezzanine. Somehow, she had managed to catch the edge, saving herself from a near seven-meter sheer drop that would either have killed or seriously injured her. However, Hudson could see that her grip was failing.

Pushing himself up, he ran toward her, just as Tory's fingers slipped from the edge. She yelled as she accelerated downward, and Hudson reached out to catch her, but, far from the fairytale image of Tory falling neatly into his arms, the momentum flattened him like a pancake.

Tory rolled off the top of Hudson, and he groaned. He'd succeeded in breaking Tory's fall, but it felt like he'd just been power-slammed by Andre the Giant.

"You're heavier than you look," Hudson whimpered, feeling his ribs. He was sure that he'd heard at least one of them crack.

"Well, I'm just glad that you're nice and soft," Tory hit back, lying flat on her back beside him.

"Hey, I'm in great shape!" complained Hudson.

Tory leaned across him, and patted his chest. Each thump of her hand felt like an anvil dropping on his sternum. "I know..." said Tory, before kissing him. "Thanks for the catch."

Hudson smiled, "I'd say, 'any time', but honestly I'd rather not do that again." Then he noticed a crack of light coming through the wall, close to the baseboard. It hadn't been visible when he was standing up. "Hey, I think there's a room hidden back there."

Tory turned over and shuffled up to the wall, running her hand along it. "You're right, there's a seam here, and an air current." She continued to work her hands along the wall, then Hudson heard a click, before a section of the wall swung inwards. They both got up and cautiously checked the newly-revealed doorway, but there didn't appear to be any sign of more booby traps.

"I told you she was a wily old fox," said Tory, stepping inside.

The room was perhaps no bigger than a large walk-in closet, but it contained a desk with a computer console, and some storage cabinets along the walls. Hudson walked around the other side of the desk and saw two drawers built into it.

"What are the chances that Yaeger has booby-trapped these drawers?" he wondered, glancing at Tory.

"Pretty high, I'd say," Tory replied, "and based on the collapsing staircase, which was slickly done, I'd say they won't be easy to get past."

Hudson examined the desk more closely. It was old and not particularly sturdy. Walking back around the rear side, he tapped the back a few times and then rubbed his chin, thoughtfully.

"Admiring the décor?" said Tory, with more than a whiff of sarcasm.

"In a sense," answered Hudson, before holding out a hand to Tory. "Can I borrow your knife?"

Tory frowned, but removed her blade from its scabbard, flipped it over and slapped the handle into Hudson's waiting hand. "So long as you're not going to stab me with it," she said, before folding her arms to see what Hudson had in mind.

Hudson then pressed the blade through a gap in the panel behind the desk drawer, and began to lever it away. The desk was in such poor condition that Hudson was quickly able to prise the wood away. Tory moved in to help, and together they pulled the back off it completely.

"See, not just a pretty face," said Hudson, handing Tory back her knife.

Tory took it and slid the blade back into its sheath. "Pretty impressive," she admitted, though she had a curious air of smug superiority about her. Tory then rested her hand next to a switch on the wall. "Or you could have just disabled all the devices with the master off-switch," she added, tapping the switch panel with her forefinger.

Hudson laughed, "Did you switch that off before or after I levered open the desk?" he wondered, but Tory just flashed her eyes mysteriously at him.

Leaving Tory to her gloating, Hudson leaned inside the desk and began to rummage through the contents of the drawers. "Bingo," he said, cautiously pulling out a cigar box from the clutter and holding it in front of him.

"Careful, Hudson, the traps in the garage are off, but she could still have rigged something in that box," warned Tory.

However, Hudson had not come this far only to be stopped by a dusty, old cigar box. He took a deep breath, held it, and then committed himself, cautiously prising open the lid of the box. He then squinted his eyes mostly shut, in case something nasty exploded from inside it, but to his relief there was nothing, except the creak of the rusted metal hinge. Lifting the lid fully, he found what he was looking for, but straight away, he knew something was wrong.

"Shit, this is only part of it." Hudson said, lifting the crystal fragment out of the box. "It looks like it has been broken in half somehow."

Tory looked at the crystal and seemed to have an epiphany. "Griff and I had what you might call a strong disagreement while heading to Chrome One," she said, cagily. "That device Cutler stole from your ship got shot up. It must have split the crystal in the process."

"If that's the case then where the hell is the other half?" Hudson said, throwing the box onto the desk.

Tory shrugged, "Best guess is that Cutler or Griff still has it," she suggested. "It makes sense. Even half a crystal could sell for a lot of credits, to someone who doesn't know any different."

Hudson nodded, "Right, but that just puts us back at square one, needing to find those slippery bastards again."

Tory thought for a moment. "If they did go back to Earth, there are a few bolt holes Cutler might use," she said, "but I'll need to do some digging first."

Hudson slipped the crystal fragment into the secret compartment in his leather jacket, then turned the computer console on the desk to face him. "We have to assume he's either sold it, or lost it," he said, switching the computer on. "Which means it's back to plan B."

Tory watched as Hudson brought up a jump map of the nearby portals. "And plan B is?..."

Hudson quickly marked a sequence of jumps from Mars to one of the more distant CET portal worlds. "We go relic hunting, and find some more crystal fragments, so that Morphus can recombine a complete crystal."

Tory peered at the screen and frowned as she noted the planet that Hudson had selected. "Why Brahms Three? There are at least a dozen less shittier shitholes we could go to."

"Sure, but they're getting fewer by the hour," cautioned Hudson, wondering how many more planets the great ship had destroyed during their time on Mars. "Goliath is working its way closer to the solar system, which puts Brahms Three in its path. And there's someone still on that sweaty little world that I owe a debt to."

"Your bartender friend, right?" said Tory, and Hudson nodded. Tory raised her eyebrows and sighed, "Fine, Brahms Three it is. But you'll have to remind your friend not to shoot me on sight. We didn't part on the best of terms, if I remember rightly."

"I'll do my best," said Hudson, smiling. Then he went to turn off the computer console, before noticing there was an emergency news alert. He switched to it, and the screen displayed a bulletin detailing Goliath's latest incursion.

"The OPW planets have all been destroyed, or the populations wiped out by the seed ships," said Hudson, his mouth going dry as he spoke. He looked at Tory. "Goliath has already turned towards the solar system, and is attacking the outer CET portal worlds en route."

"Then it looks like we'd better go relic hunting, pretty damn quickly," said Tory.

Hudson shut down the computer and headed out of Yaeger's hidden office room. He remained vigilant for signs of the Council as he moved back to the door of the garage, but when he got there, he noticed that Tory wasn't behind him. He peered around the garage space and spotted her, dragging a fuel barrel underneath Cutler's FS-31. With the traps now disabled, Tory was free to roam the garage without fear of a gruesome surprise.

"Tory, what are you doing?" Hudson called out to her, "We don't have time for this."

Tory tipped some of the fuel on to the floor underneath the FS-31, then dragged a second barrel alongside the first. "I don't care if Goliath is in orbit above Mars right now," Tory said, moving to a cabinet and searching through it. "I'm still going to blow this ship to hell."

Tory continued to rummage until she found what she was looking for. Walking back over towards Hudson, he finally managed to see what the object was. "You're serious?" he said, looking at the welding torch in Tory's hand.

Tory lit the torch and threw it at the fuel barrels. It hit the metal deck and skidded squarely into the middle of them. She turned back to Hudson, who was standing in front of the door, and threw her arms out wide. "Well, what the hell are you waiting for? Run!"

Hudson scrambled out of the door and set off at a sprint away from the garage. Tory caught up with him a few seconds later, as the fuel ignited and the tanks exploded. The detonation blew out the front of the building, throwing them both to the ground.

Hudson groaned again, and rolled onto his back, before sitting up. Tory grabbed his shoulder and hauled herself up alongside him. Through the now blown-open front of the garage, they could see the FS-31, collapsed in a burning heap on the deck.

"That felt *really* good," said Tory, smiling.

Hudson rubbed his aching head, "Speak for yourself," he said, as the garage's fire suppression systems kicked in. "But I'm glad you found it cathartic." Hudson noted that it certainly seemed to have lifted Tory's spirits, but he wished she'd chosen a less destructive way to iron out her frustrations. "From now on, though, how about you just stick to intimidating and shooting people, and not blowing things up?"

CHAPTER 8

Logan Griff cautiously opened the door of the pre-fab office building, below which was the bolt hole he and Wash were hiding in. He pushed the door open a touch wider, and peered outside onto Swinsler's lot. It was the early evening in San Francisco, and the warm autumn air was clear of fog.

"Are you going outside or not?" asked Jane Wash, tapping her foot impatiently. "If Cutler was waiting for us out there, he'd have emptied a magazine through the door by now."

Griff glared back at Wash. As his commanding officer, he'd grown accustomed to her spiky and cantankerous moods, but usually his time spent with her was mercifully short. Forced to endure hours alone with Wash in the confines of the bolt hole, he'd felt like strangling her.

"Best to be cautious where Cutler is concerned," he replied, but Wash just tutted and barged past him, flinging the door open in the process, and stepping outside.

"See, no Cutler," crowed Wash, indicating to the empty shipyard lot. "He knows he has something we need, so when he's ready, he'll make himself known."

Griff also now stepped outside, satisfied that if Cutler was waiting around to kill them, Wash would already be dead. Part of him wished that Cutler had gunned her down then and there, but he knew he still needed Wash to escape. He plucked a cigarette out of the black packet in his shirt pocket, and lit it. "You're assuming he hasn't already sold or traded the crystal," he said, blowing out a plume of dark smoke. "He's pretty desperate now."

Wash walked up to Griff and pulled the cigarette out of his mouth, before placing it into her own. "Then you'd better find out if he has or not," she said, before drawing deeply on the stick.

Griff glowered at her, and slid out another smoke from the packet. "Well, that's where we're going now, isn't it?" he said, though it came off sounding a little more petulant than he'd intended.

"Right now, all I'm hearing is your jaw flapping," replied Wash, continuing in her ill-tempered mood. "So, lead the way, Inspector Griff..."

Griff brushed past Wash and headed out towards the rusted iron gates of the shipyard lot. He then saw Swinsler waving at him from inside his own office pre-fab, his round face offering a fake smile, but he ignored him. Swinsler was only slightly less irritating than Wash was, and Griff's mood was already stormy enough. Then he heard the door of the pre-fab open, and rolled his eyes as the round little man ran out to greet him.

"Good evening, Inspector Griff," said Swinsler, sounding as if he was gearing up to sell him a ship. "I trust all is well with the accommodations?"

"Yeah, they're fine," replied Griff, before glancing back at Wash, "Apart from the company, anyway."

Swinsler turned his round spectacles towards Wash, who was following a few meters behind Griff, but she was also seemingly trying to ignore the dealer. "Well, if you need anything, be sure to let me know!" Swinsler intoned.

Griff noticed the dealer was holding an epaper in this right hand. He stopped, reached down and plucked the device from Swinsler's chubby fingers. "I need to borrow this, if you don't mind," said Griff, though he hadn't phrased it as a question, and didn't wait for Swinsler to provide an answer, either. Then he clicked his fingers, remembering something else he needed. "Oh, and if you can lend me some hardbucks, that would be great," he added. It was a thirty-minute walk into Bayview from the lot, and he didn't want to spend that amount of time forced to endure Wash's idle chit-chat and insults. He also didn't want to pay for a transport with credits, which would risk leaving a digital fingerprint for the Council to trace.

Swinsler hesitated, then reluctantly pulled out a small bundle of notes. "Well, I suppose I could..." he said, reticent to hand them over.

Griff snatched the entire bundle from his hand, "Just stick it on her tab," he said, nodding behind to Wash. Swinsler stammered an incoherent reply, but Griff had already walked away.

Outside the gates of the shipyard, Griff managed to flag down a passing ground transport. He opened the door and slid across the rear seat to the other side, leaving the door open for Wash.

"Such a gentleman," said Wash, as she got in and closed the door. Griff didn't acknowledge her snide remark, but he was pleased that he'd manage to aggravate her.

"Do you know the Antiques and Curiosity Shoppe, up in Bayview?" Griff asked the driver, who nodded.

"Are you guys antiques dealers then?" the transport driver asked, trying to be friendly. He frowned at Wash, and added, "Hey, you look familiar. Are you an actress or something?"

Wash rolled her eyes at him, "Just shut up and drive," she said, shutting the man down with her usual charm. The driver visibly recoiled, and started driving. To Griff, Wash asked, "A curiosity shop? These IDs need to be real, not novelty items, I do hope you realize that?"

Griff had turned on the epaper and was busy scanning the headlines, but Wash's dumb question prompted him to look up. "You know, while you were sitting on your scrawny ass in your big office chair, polishing your rank slides, I've actually been out in the real world," he said, before looking back at the epaper. "I know what I'm doing, so why don't you just sit tight and shut up for once?" He expected an explosion from Wash in response, but to his surprise, she actually sounded impressed.

"Well, well, it's about time you grew a pair," Wash replied, turning to look out of the window. "I was beginning to wonder if you were as wet as that simpering moron, Powell."

Wash turned back to Griff, perhaps expecting him to rise to the bait, but Griff was scowling down at the epaper.

"Today's comic strips a bit too highbrow for you?" Wash asked, snootily.

Griff slid the privacy glass shut, and made sure the microphones in the cabin were off. Then he looked up at Wash and held out the epaper to her. "The CET has issued a warrant for your arrest," he said, as Wash snatched the epaper from his hand and scowled at it, furiously. "Looks like the higher-ups have thrown you to the wolves," Griff added, trying hard not to sound too pleased. "The official statement from the RGF is that you acted unilaterally, and that your attempt to take control of a portal world is in breach of yada, yada, yada regulations. You get the picture." Then he reached over and pointed to a section of the article. "There's a photo of you too, which is likely why the cabby thinks you're famous. Unless he just likes your ass, which I doubt..."

Wash scowled at Griff, and hurriedly scrolled through the article, before skim-reading several others. "Your name is listed too," she said, shooting a glance across to him.

"Yeah, I know," replied Griff, grumpily. All the article confirmed was that he was stuck with his asshole former commanding officer for the time being.

The ground transport pulled up to the sidewalk, and the driver tapped on the privacy glass. Griff slid it back.

"This is the place," the driver said pointing to the storefront outside. "There's a credit scanner in the back there for the fare." Griff got out a fifty-dollar hardbuck note and thrust it through the window. The driver took it, staring at it almost in wonder. "Wow, I don't see these much nowadays. I can't give you any change, though, and this is worth way more than the fare cost."

Griff opened the door and stepped out, before leaning back inside. "Just call it a tip for having to put up with Princess pain-in-the-ass, there," he said, looking at Wash.

Wash also got out and joined Griff on the sidewalk. "Don't push your luck, Inspector," she snarled at Griff. "Just remember who you're talking to."

Griff laughed, and grabbed the door handle of the Antiques and Curiosity Shoppe. "I know who I'm talking to, former-Superintendent Wash," he hit back, adding extra emphasis on the word 'former'. "The truth is that you're nothing more than a wanted criminal now, just like me," he added, pushing open the door. "So, you'd better get used to treating me with a bit more respect."

Griff entered the small store, not bothering to hold the door open for Wash, and walked up to the counter. Wash appeared behind him a few seconds later, wearing an expression like thunder.

"I'll be with you in a second," came the haughty voice of Cortland, from somewhere in the back office. The crooked artefacts dealer then appeared and the supercilious smile instantly fell from his face. "Logan Griff..."

Griff frowned, "We haven't seen each other in years," he said, instantly suspicious, "yet, you seemed to recognize me pretty easily."

Cortland reached underneath the counter, but Griff immediately pulled his weapon on him. "Not so fast; hands where I can see them!" he snarled, aiming the barrel at the dealer's head.

"Calm yourself, Mr. Griff, I am merely ensuring that we are not disturbed," protested Cortland. "I have learned my lesson when it comes to your sort."

"Our sort?" snorted Griff. "What the hell is that supposed to mean?"

"May I?" replied Cortland, indicating to the counter, and Griff nodded.

Then the dealer hit a button, locking the door and tinting the windows black. Griff lowered his pistol, as Cortland's hands reappeared and rested on the counter top.

"Let's just say, you're not the only wanted criminals that have entered my premises recently," Cortland continued, appearing more at ease.

"Cutler Wendell was here?" asked Griff.

Cortland nodded. "Yes, and he said you would likely show up too."

Wash immediately drew her weapon, moved away from the window and covered the door. Griff became twitchier too, holding his weapon ready and moving so that he could see through into the back-office area.

"He's not here, if that's what you're concerned about," said Cortland, raising his voice a little to recapture their attention. "He offered to sell me an alien crystal fragment, but I declined."

"Why?" asked Griff, genuinely surprised that a snake like Cortland wouldn't take advantage of Cutler's desperate situation.

"Is that a serious question?" asked Cortland, with an even haughtier air than Wash usually managed. "The CET and MP authorities are all searching for it. It's just about the hottest piece of contraband in the galaxy right now, and I want nothing to do with it."

"Great," moaned Griff, realizing that his idea of the crystal as an insurance policy would now be more of an albatross around his neck.

"However, Cutler also gave me a message to relay to you," Cortland added, enigmatically.

Griff lowered his weapon again and moved back to the counter. "What message?"

"May I?" asked Cortland, as he again went to slide his hand under the counter.

"Slowly..." said Griff, watching the dealer like a hawk.

Cortland then brought up a small datapad, which he placed on the counter top, before sliding it over in front of Griff. "He said that he will exchange the item he took from you – the crystal, I presume – for the shuttlecraft," Cortland continued. "He then said he would consider all debts paid, and his business relationship with you to be terminated, permanently."

Griff huffed a laugh, "An interesting turn of phrase," he commented.

"The location for the rendezvous is in the pad," Cortland continued, "You can also use this device to message him the meeting time directly. The link is secure and encrypted."

Griff picked up the pad and switched it on. It showed the site for the rendezvous. "The location is up in Point Reyes," Griff said, glancing over to Wash. "Flat, and in the middle of nowhere. The perfect spot for a trade, or more likely an ambush."

Wash moved beside Griff and snatched the pad from his hands. Griff felt like shoving it down her throat.

"There are two of us, and one of him," said Wash, studying the location. "I believe he'll do the trade, as promised; it's in his interest, since he cannot move the crystal any other way."

Griff shook his head, "But neither can we, so what use is it?" he countered. "We need a shuttle more than we need a smashed-up crystal that all the damn CET and MP military are hunting for."

"I have my own ship," said Wash, before adding snobbishly, "which is considerably more refined than that wreck of a shuttle you arrived in." Then she switched off the datapad and handed it back to Griff. "And if the CET and MP want this crystal so badly, then it gives us something to negotiate with."

Griff had to admit she had a point. Though he still suspected Cutler would try to double-cross them. "Fine, we'll do it your way," replied Griff. "But we'll still need the fake IDs, just in case this all goes south, which I'm sure it will."

Cortland's face suddenly lit up. "You are in need of Counterfeit IDs?"

"Real ones, not novelty items," Wash added, shooting a snarky look at Griff. Then she jabbed her finger at Cortland, "And they have to be top quality – no mistakes."

"Of course!" beamed Cortland, "You've come to the right place! If you'd like to come this way." Then Cortland disappeared into the back-office room.

Griff turned to Wash, and indicated for her to go first, "After you, ma'am," he said, with a bow like a courtier.

Wash walked up to him, so close that he could smell the tobacco on her breath. "Be careful, Griff, I'm warning you," she said with a restrained malice, before walking around the counter and into the back room.

CHAPTER 9

The Orion's upgraded, alien propulsion system had got them close to Brahms Three in unfeasibly quick time, but the final transit had taken longer than Hudson had expected. This had been down to the high volume of traffic heading through the portal in the opposite direction. People were now abandoning Brahms Three, and all the other portal worlds, in huge numbers, all desperately trying to flee from Goliath's relentless advance. However, Hudson knew that there was no chance of escape; the great ship was merely herding its prey into a more concentrated space. Left unchecked, Goliath would eventually destroy every inhabited planet, while its seed ships would pursue and kill every human being in the galaxy.

In some ways, Hudson envied those running away, because they were ignorant of the true scale of the threat. Hudson, however, was burdened with the raw, unfiltered reality of what was to come, if they couldn't stop Goliath.

"Are you sure this friend of yours will still be there?" asked Tory, as the Orion finally completed its entry into the planet's sweaty atmosphere, and started to descend towards the scavenger town. "I'm picking up dozens of ships departing the surface, and the spaceport is almost deserted."

Hudson checked the navigation scanner, which confirmed what Tory had said. "I doubt she'd leave, at least not until the last second. As much as Brahms Three is a dump to most people, that bar is her home." Then he noticed that a few ships had landed just outside the checkpoint district, and that the RGF outpost was shut down. "It looks like we're not the only ones planning a last-minute relic hunt," he commented. "The RGF has already bailed out, which means it will be easy to smuggle relics off site, without paying any taxes."

"Opportunistic hunters are the most dangerous," cautioned Tory, as she circled the Orion around the scavenger town. "We should expect trouble."

Hudson nodded, peering down at the small city, which had been built almost entirely from modified shipping containers. Now that their altitude was lower, he could see people running in the streets, carrying boxes and bags. In several places there was fighting, both hand-to-hand, and with firearms.

"This place is going to hell," said Hudson, as Tory descended towards the Orion's private docking stand. "Just getting to the Landing Strip without being shot at will be a challenge."

The Orion touched down on the surface, and Tory shut down the engines. She unclipped her harness and swiveled the chair to face Hudson. "Are you sure you still want to do this?" she asked, though she phrased the question neutrally, not intending to convey her opinion either way. "As you said, the crystal is the priority. And we don't know how long it will be before Goliath gets here."

Deep down, Hudson knew that Tory was right. The smart thing to do would be to land near the RGF checkpoint perimeter, and head straight into the wreck. But if Ma was still in the town, and he left without knowing if she was okay, he'd never forgive himself.

"Martina dragged me out of a hole when I was ready to sink deeper into it," said Hudson, frankly. "She didn't abandon me, and I can't do it to her. But, you're right about Goliath. Perhaps you should hunt for the crystal fragment in the wreck, and leave Ma to me."

Tory shook her head, "Whatever we do, we do it together," she replied, with the firmness Hudson had grown accustomed to. "If she's important to you, then she's important to me."

Hudson smiled, "As a bonus, she does make great whiskey."

Tory got up and grabbed the 1873 Winchester that was hanging over the back of her seat. "Then let's make sure we liberate some of that too," she replied, before slinging the rifle over her shoulder.

Hudson and Tory cautiously exited the Orion, as more ships took off and blasted away from the scavenger town. Weapons drawn and ready, they moved towards the main street outside the spaceport. Other than fleeing, the main occupation of those who were still in the town appeared to be looting. The well-stocked Scavenger's Paradise relic hunter store seemed to be a popular target. The tills had all been abandoned and emptied, and the humorless armed security guards that defended the entrance had gone. Tory tapped Hudson on the shoulder and then headed towards the door.

"I'm not sure now is the right time to go shopping," Hudson said, as a looter ran past Tory, carrying an armful of goods.

"If we're going hunting then I'm going to need a few more supplies," she replied, "and a *lot* more ammunition."

Hudson reluctantly followed her through the door, dodging more fleeing looters. Tory seemed unconcerned with the chaos unfolding inside. She strolled casually along the aisles as if simply grabbing some milk and a newspaper on a Sunday morning.

"Do these stores even carry ammunition for your antique weapons?" asked Hudson, pressing himself against a shelf rack as a woman charged past with a trolley.

Tory found a backpack on the floor – probably dropped by another frantic looter – and began filling it up.

"Plenty of hunters and mercs are fans of the classics," Tory replied, throwing some items into the bag. "And since the cartridges cost a lot more, these places tend to stock them and add a nice markup." Then she found the section containing the boxes of .44-40 she was looking for. She flashed her eyes at Hudson, smiling more broadly than he'd ever seen her smile before.

"Hold this open," she said, handing Hudson the bag. She then began to dump boxes of the ammo inside, before finally taking the bag back.

"We're going hunting inside a wreck, not joining Custer's Last Stand..." said Hudson, peering in at the vast quantity of ammo that Tory had thrown into the bag.

"Custer didn't do so well at the Little Bighorn," replied Tory, "I don't intend our last stand to be so ill-fated."

Hudson then spotted a box of ammo for his compact pistol, and added it to the bag too. Tory looked at it, and raised an eyebrow at Hudson.

"Are you actually planning to use that, or are you still preferring to fight with harsh words?"

"Intimidating and shooting people is your job, remember?" said Hudson, "But there's no harm in being prepared..."

They finished grabbing the supplies they needed for the hunt and turned back towards the exit. However, they had only made it a few paces before a trio of hunters turned a corner and blocked their aisle. Hudson was about to apologize and politely move past, but there was something about the lead man that was familiar. He was still struggling to put a name to the face, when Tory answered the question for him.

"Rex Kove," said Tory, quickly slinging the bag, and placing her hand onto her six-shooter. "I thought it smelled bad in here."

Then Hudson remembered who the thick-set man was. Rex 'Tombstone' Kove was the relic hunter he'd encountered in the wreck on Brahms Three, the first time he'd met Tory. Hudson remembered it was an encounter that didn't go so well for the burly relic hunter.

"I'm glad you haven't forgotten me," said Rex, a smile emphasizing the lines in his craggy face. He was dressed the same as Hudson remembered, with a vintage DPM combat vest, over the top of a tight black tank top. His arms, which were folded across his broad chest, looked even bigger than the first time he'd seen them. "Because I haven't forgotten that you shot me with a tranq dart, and then stole everything I had!" Rex added, bitterly.

"Stop your whining, you're still alive, aren't you?" replied Tory, showing no remorse. "You have Hudson to thank for that, remember?"

Rex now looked at Hudson, and though it took a few moments, the muscular relic hunter finally recognized him. "That's right, you were her pet clobber, weren't you?" he said, and without giving Hudson a chance to answer, added, "I knew you two were working together."

"Do you want something, Rex?" Tory cut in, sounding bored. "Because the smell is really starting to sting my eyes now."

Rex took a few steps forward, and Hudson saw his two sons rest their hands on their pistols. "I want back what you stole from me," said Rex, peering down at Tory, "and I'm going to get it."

Tory scowled and wafted a hand in front of her nose, as if Rex had just broken wind. "Haven't you heard of showers?" she said, adding a fake cough for effect. "The deodorant is on aisle five, by the way."

Rex's lined face scrunched into a confused scowl, "This place doesn't sell deodorant."

Tory shook her head, "So you're thick as pig shit, as well as stinking like it."

Despite himself, Hudson laughed, drawing an angry glower from Rex.

Tory then slid past the mighty frame of Rex Kove, and walked up to his two sons. "Move out of my way, pumpkins," she said, and the young hunters parted, as ordered. Tory breezed past them and then turned back to Rex. "I'd like to say it was nice seeing you again, Rex, but that would be a lie," she added, before strolling away.

Hudson turned to follow, but Rex grabbed him and held him back. His massive hand closed almost entirely around Hudson's forearm. "Don't get too attached to your little girlfriend," he snarled. "Because she ain't making it off this rock, without paying me what I'm owed."

Hudson shook off his powerful grip, and squared off against the bigger man. "I saved your ass once," he said, reprising his tough guy 'relic hunter' persona for the first time since his last hunt. "Don't expect me to do it again. I strongly suggest that you stay out of our way."

Then Hudson strode off confidently, stepping through the two sons, who parted, this time without being ordered to. He met Tory on the steps of the Scavenger's Paradise. She was filling her webbing pouches and ammo carrier with the new .44-40s she had just acquired.

"He's going to be a problem, isn't he?" said Hudson, as another two looters raced past on the street, chased by a man with a baseball bat. The town was going crazy.

Tory nodded, "Yes, he is. And Rex won't be the only asshole hunter in that wreck that's going to cause us headaches."

Hudson squeezed his eyes shut and rubbed his temples. Just reaching the Landing Strip bar would put them at risk of catching a stray bullet. He knew what they had to do, but hated having to make the choice.

"Okay, change of plans; we go to the wreck first," he said, firmly. "We can't risk any delay, like you said. We find those fragments and the crystal recombiner device, and then come back for Ma, if there's still time."

Tory frowned, "Are you sure? I'll back you up either way."

"I know you will," said Hudson, smiling back at Tory. "But stopping Goliath has to come first. I don't like it, but it's the right thing to do."

"I'm not used to doing the right thing," sighed Tory.

Hudson smiled again. "Well, for someone so inexperienced at it, you're doing pretty well so far."

Tory got up and offered Hudson her hand. "Okay then, one last hunt."

Hudson took her hand, and she pulled him up. "One last hunt. Let's make it one to remember."

CHAPTER 10

To save time, Hudson and Tory had returned to the Orion and flown it directly to the crashed Revocater, before setting it down on the hull. Ordinarily, a couple of RGF Patrol Craft would have forcefully chased them off way before that point, but the few RGF officers that had remained were too preoccupied trying to police the hunters that were already leaving the wreck.

Hudson had chosen a landing site as close as possible to the area indicated on the map Morphus had given him. However, even from their advantageous starting position, they were still limited by the need to find a suitable entry-point into the Revocater.

"Assuming we can navigate a fairly direct route, it shouldn't take long to reach the navigation hub," said Hudson, studying the map on the datapad.

Hudson was wearing a rucksack and carrying the climbing gear, while Tory had attached an assortment of tools and gizmos to her webbing pouches. The 1873 Winchester, which was now rarely parted from Tory, was also slung over her back.

They had managed to climb down unassisted to a ledge inside the Revocater's outer hull. Now Tory was attaching the last of three anchors into the alien metal, so they could drop into one of the ship's labyrinthine corridors. She fed the ropes through the anchors, and handed one to Hudson.

"We're lucky that the crash ripped open the hull so close to where we need to be," said Tory, getting ready to descend. "The sooner we're in and out of this thing, the better."

"You'll get no argument from me," replied Hudson, as he peered down into the fissure. He guessed it was probably thirty meters to the inner corridor from where they were. "Reaching this point from one of the established entrances would have taken a good couple of hours; maybe more."

Tory nodded and started to lower herself down. "That's true, but this section will still have been well trodden by previous hunters," she said, dropping further into the chasm. "So, we still need to be careful of other crews that may already be in here. And of booby traps too."

Tory reached the bottom and unclipped, then Hudson followed her down. He also unclipped, then removed the datapad from his pocket and studied the map again. Helpfully, it indicated their current position, and even showed a route to where they needed to be.

"Shit, what I wouldn't have given for this a few years ago," said Tory, looking at the map over Hudson's shoulder.

"I don't know how it's doing it, but it sort of takes the fun out of the hunt, don't you think?" replied Hudson. He then orientated himself and found the corridor they needed to venture down.

"Who the hell does this for fun?" snorted Tory. "The only fun part is counting your profits and the number of bullets you dodged at the end of each hunt."

Hudson laughed and said, "Come on, where's your sense of adventure?"

Tory unslung the Winchester and cocked it. "I left it back on Sapphire Alpha, just before Goliath destroyed the planet," came the tongue-in-cheek reply. Then she gestured for Hudson to lead the way. "After you, adventure-lover..."

Their progress towards the navigation hub of the Revocater was aided by the many established bridges and ladders that other hunters had put in place over the years. However, not all of the human additions to the Revocater were designed to be helpful, and Tory also needed to disarm three booby traps within the first few hundred meters. Eventually, they came to a large chamber with a curious hexagonal mass in the center. Metal conduits connected it to the floor and ceiling, giving it an hourglass-like shape. The far wall of the chamber was directly adjacent to where they needed to be, but where the map showed a route between the two spaces, Hudson saw only a solid metal bulkhead.

"This must be the part where Morphus said a corporeal couldn't get through," said Hudson, showing the datapad to Tory. "We need to find these channels it said would lead inside."

Tory and Hudson carefully surveyed the wall, each starting at opposite ends.

"We're lucky this section is intact," commented Tory, as she worked her way across. "I've been to this area before, in other wrecks, and it has always been totally caved in." Then she suddenly stopped, and called out, "Hey, over here. I think I've found something."

Hudson hurried over and saw that Tory was examining a narrow, circular opening in the wall. He shone his torchlight inside, but the conduit didn't appear to extend all the way through the bulkhead. Instead, it cut across further in towards the center. Hudson had a thought, and moved over to the corresponding position on the opposite side of the wall.

"There's one here too," he said, finding another narrow opening. The second conduit also jinked towards the center a short distance inside.

"I've seen similar openings in other parts of the ship," said Tory, who had come to investigate the second hole. "I thought nothing of them. I guess no hunter ever did."

Tory unzipped the side pocket of Hudson's backpack and removed the cannonball-like device Morphus had given them. Hudson frowned at the object, which Morphus had called a 'short-range matter demolecularizer', and turned his concerned eyes to Tory. "What did I tell you about not blowing anything else up?"

"Where's your sense of adventure?" replied Tory, smiling roguishly. Then she crouched down by the opening to the conduit, and got ready to activate the device. "We have no idea what the blast radius of this thing is, so once I pop it in the hole, I suggest we run like hell to the other side of this chamber."

Hudson nodded, wishing in hindsight that he'd asked what Morphus' definition of 'short-range' was. Tory then twisted the small metal sphere, causing the trench around its diameter to light up red, before hurriedly pushing it into the hole. They both got up to run, however Hudson noticed the device had barely moved through the conduit.

"Tory, hold up!" Hudson called out.

"Hold up?!" cried Tory, "Are you crazy?!"

Hudson rushed over to Tory and grabbed the rifle off her shoulder. "The damn thing is stuck," he shouted, rushing back to the opening.

"Well, I don't think shooting it will help!" cried Tory, her voice almost frantic.

Hudson thrust the end of the rifle into the conduit and poked the metal sphere with the end of the barrel. It dislodged and began to roll freely along the channel inside.

"Run!" Hudson shouted, turning and sprinting away from the wall. Seconds later there was a pulsating throb that rose to near deafening levels, before Hudson and Tory were hit with a blast of air, throwing them to the deck.

The gust dissipated, and Hudson rolled onto his back. His ears were ringing and it felt like someone had used his head as a drum. Tory appeared above him. Her mouth was moving, but he couldn't hear anything.

"I can't hear you," he answered, though from the startled look on Tory's face, he guessed he must have shouted the words at her. Slowly the ringing subsided and he could start to make out other sounds.

"I said, where the hell did you get the idea to do that?" Tory repeated, helping him up. "Using my rifle as a poker, I mean."

"Haven't you ever played pool in a bar?" replied Hudson, brushing himself off.

Tory shrugged, "No, there are only two things I do in bars – drink and fight," she answered, and Hudson knew she wasn't joking, or exaggerating. Then Tory's eyes widened, as she looked back to the metal bulkhead, or at least what remained of it. She let out a low whistle and added, "That little alien gizmo certainly packed a hell of a punch."

Hudson looked over to the far wall and saw that a large, perfectly round hole had appeared in it. It was like a giant beach ball had been inflated inside the middle of the bulkhead, vaporizing the metal as it grew larger.

Hudson handed the Winchester rifle back to Tory and went over to inspect the new opening. He cautiously stepped through the spherical hole, which, remarkably, was completely cool to the touch, and discovered an entirely new chamber, unseen and untouched for thousands of years. Unlike the space he'd come from, which already had lights in place from years of earlier hunts, the new room was dark and cold. However, from what little illumination filtered through the opening, Hudson estimated that it was roughly the same size as a basketball court. And, as he ventured further inside, it also seemed to be partially collapsed.

"Shit, it looks like this section has taken some damage after all," said Tory, shining her torch through the opening. "I hope we can still find what we need."

Hudson sighed, and glanced back at Tory. "I guess there's only one way to find out..."

CHAPTER 11

Hudson pulled on a headtorch and continued deeper inside the Revocater's navigation hub. Tory caught up with him a few seconds later, and shone the beam of her more powerful flashlight further into the room.

"The damage doesn't actually look too bad," said Tory, focusing the column of light at the crumpled metal panels at the far end of the room. "We might have struck gold after all." Then something glinted in the beam of her torchlight, and she moved closer to inspect it. "Hudson, here!" she called over to him, illuminating the object with the torch.

Hudson hurried over and saw a hexagonal tower extending from the floor to the partially-collapsed ceiling. It was positioned just behind a strange-looking metal pod that looked a bit like a witch's cauldron, except the material was slightly golden, rather than a necrotic black. It reminded Hudson of something he'd seen before. At first, he couldn't place where, but then it dawned on him. "I saw something similar to this in Morphus' shuttle," said Hudson, running his hand over the smooth, golden metal. "This pod is bigger, but it looks more or less the same."

Hudson then peered into the pod, and saw a large hexagonal pyramid that seemed to extend into the deck below their feet. It was surrounded by a pool of liquid that also had a strange golden color, similar to how Morphus appeared during its transformations. However, the liquid metal in the pod was dull and lifeless, compared to Morphus' shimmering, iridescent form. He remembered that Morphus had said the navigation hub was where they would also find the remains of the Revocater pilot.

"I think we're looking at this ship's version of Morphus," said Hudson. He suddenly felt a powerful swell of sorrow rise up out of nowhere, and he almost teared up. They were fighting to save humanity, but Hudson had forgotten that Morphus was already the last of its kind. They'd merely taken its help for granted, and never considered how Morphus might feel. In the beginning, Hudson wasn't sure whether the alien AI experienced emotions at all, at least in the way humans did, but the longer he had spent with the entity, the more real it had appeared to him.

Tory looked into the pod, then noticed Hudson's forlorn expression. "Hey, this one is long dead," she said, a little too coldly for Hudson's liking. Then she redeemed herself, "But Morphus can still live on, if we find this damn gadget and get out of here in one piece."

Hudson pulled out the datapad, and checked the information Morphus had added about the crystal recombiner. He looked at the hexagonal tower just behind the pod, and the image and description seemed to match.

"That's it right there," said Hudson, pointing to the tower.

"How the hell are we supposed to get that back to the ship?" said Tory, examining the structure more closely. "I doubt we could carry it more than a couple of hundred meters."

"We don't need the whole thing, just the main crystal chamber," replied Hudson, showing the image on the datapad to Tory. Then he shrugged, "But I've no idea how to get it out."

Suddenly, there was a noise outside the navigation hub, and they both froze. Tory held the Winchester ready, and moved closer to the opening. "That blast could have brought some unwanted attention," she called back to Hudson, in hushed tones. "We need to hurry. I'll cover us, while you try to figure out how to remove that chamber."

Hudson started to swiftly inspect the tower, looking for panels that could be detached, or other compartments. Tory had stealthily moved over to the circular hole in the wall, and taken up a defensive position with the Winchester.

Come on, damn it, there must be some way into this thing, Hudson thought, but it seemed perfectly uniform. Then he moved his hands over a section of the tower, and the skin on his wrist suddenly glowed. It was where Morphus had augmented his body to act as an ID fob for the Orion. Slowly, he moved his wrist back, until it glowed more brightly again. *Is it reacting to the crystal somehow?* Hudson wondered. It was just a guess, but it was all he had to go on.

Hudson focused his search on that section of the tower, and finally spotted a thin seam in the metal. Pressing onto it, a panel popped open, then swung upwards. Inside, there was an object about the size of a shoebox, connected by four metal tubes. It certainly looked like the object Morphus had stored in the datapad's memory, Hudson thought.

"I think I have it," Hudson called over to Tory, but she hurriedly turned to him and pressed a finger to her lips. Using hand signals, she then indicated that there were four hunters outside.

Shit, it could be Rex, or worse! Hudson guessed. With renewed urgency, he began trying to wrestle the tubes off the crystal recombination chamber.

Suddenly three gunshots rang out, and Hudson saw Tory pull back behind cover.

"I don't think they're very friendly," Tory called over to Hudson, before firing three shots in return. "Any chance you can hurry up?"

Hudson finally managed to dislodge the tubes, and slid the box out of the tower. It was translucent, and Hudson could see fragments of crystal rattling around inside. It wasn't much, and he doubted it would be enough for Morphus to recombine an entire crystal from the fragment they already had. However, unless they could find Cutler and Griff, before Goliath arrived in the solar system, it would have to do.

Quickly sliding the box into his rucksack, he then drew his pistol and moved to the other side of the opening from Tory. More shots rang out, and Hudson heard the rounds ping off the walls inside the chamber.

"Do you have it?" asked Tory, and Hudson nodded. "Then I'm done messing around with these assholes." She reached into a webbing pouch, and pulled out what looked like a grenade.

"Hey, no blowing stuff up, remember?" said Hudson, but Tory had already activated the device.

"Just cover your ears and shut your eyes," she shouted, before tossing the object through the opening.

Hudson quickly did as Tory said, and a couple of seconds later there was a detonation outside.

"Let's move!" Tory cried out, running through the opening.

Hudson followed, and saw the four hunters, all lying on the ground, stunned.

"It was only a glimmer!" Tory called back, answering Hudson's unspoken question. Though again her lips were curled into a roguish smirk.

"You could have told me!" cried Hudson, racing after her, but then they turned onto another corridor, and almost ran straight into three more hunters.

There was a second's hesitation, before the lead hunter raised his weapon. Tory's reactions were equal to the hunter's, and she deflected the pistol with the butt of the Winchester. Hudson then darted forward and instinctively pistol-whipped the next nearest hunter over the head. The man fell, knocking into his partner, and Hudson advanced, denying the final hunter an opportunity to get a shot off.

Hudson attacked, but his blow was parried, and he felt a knee thump into his ribs. Grimacing, he was then thrown back against the wall and hit with two solid punches. Hudson fought back, grabbing the hunter's jacket and shoving him away, before driving his elbow into the man's face. His opponent yelped, and Hudson followed up with two more hard shots to the gut, which put the hunter out of commission.

He turned back to Tory, but her assailant was also now on the floor, blood gushing from his nose. Then angry cries filtered down the corridor, from the direction of the navigation hub.

"Quickly, they might still come after us!" Hudson shouted. Then, as if on cue, one of the original four hunters appeared at the end of the corridor. Hudson quickly fired two rounds, driving the female hunter back into cover, then he ran, harder and faster than he'd ever run in his life.

Hudson's lungs burned and muscles ached as he scrambled over the makeshift bridges that led back to where they'd entered the Revocater. Heavy bootsteps continued to follow them, and Tory periodically halted to fire shots back along their route, driving their pursuers into cover.

"They're persistent, I'll give them that!" shouted Tory over the crack of more gunfire. Hudson reached the ropes that they'd set up to climb inside the ship, and held one out to Tory. However, Tory simply grabbed the rope and hooked Hudson onto it. "You go first," she said, before sliding some more rounds into the Winchester from the ammo holder on its strap.

"Hey, we go together," said Hudson, not buying into the idea of leaving Tory to fend off four angry hunters by herself, but Tory shook her head.

"You have to get that relic out of here," she insisted, "I'll keep these assholes busy until you get up to the surface. Then I'm relying on you to haul my ass to safety."

Hudson glanced up through the fissure in the hull; the ascent looked considerably more difficult than the descent had been. "I'm going to need arms like Rex to pull that off..." he said, doubtfully.

"Then I'll just have to rely on your desire not to see me shot to pieces to give you the boost you need..." Tory added, before slapping him on the back, "Go, now!"

Hudson grabbed the ascender and started to climb the rope as quickly as he could. He'd barely made it ten meters before Tory started shooting. Each crack of the rifle was like an extra shot of adrenaline, pushing Hudson to climb harder and faster.

He finally reached the top and rigged a quick three-to-one raise, before calling down to Tory, "I'm ready!"

Tory popped off another couple of rounds and then clipped herself on to the rope, before shouting, "Go, go, go!"

Hudson began to pull on the rope, wishing at that moment that he really did have arms like Rex Kove. Tory slung the rifle and quickly prepared another glimmer. A hunter appeared below and fired, missing Tory by inches. Tory swung out of the hunter's firing arc, then armed the glimmer, before dropping it down the chasm. There were more angry shouts from below, then the glimmer detonated, briefly filling the darkness with a brilliant white light. It had worked; the compact stun grenade bought Hudson just enough time for Tory to reach the ledge and haul herself to safety.

Hudson collapsed on to his back, gasping for air, as more shots flew up the chasm. His arms felt like they were no longer attached to his body, as if they were molded from plasticine and merely stuck on to his shoulders. Tory quickly drew her knife and cut the ropes, before also collapsing onto her back beside Hudson.

They both lay there, panting for another full minute, until Hudson was finally able to speak again.

"I take it back," Hudson wheezed, as Tory rested her head onto his aching shoulder. "Relic hunting isn't fun at all…"

CHAPTER 12

With the crystal recombiner safely aboard the Orion, and Tory doing the flying, Hudson used the welcome lull in activity to catch up on the news feeds about Goliath. It made for grim reading. The OPW were already gone, and Elgar Five – one of the outermost CET portal worlds – had been attacked too. Reports of the alien ship's progress now put Brahms Three directly between it and Earth. Hudson knew that it was only a matter of time before Goliath showed up in the system, but despite the urgent need to get the crystal recombiner to Morphus, he still couldn't leave without knowing that Ma was safe. He owed her that much.

On their approach to the spaceport, Hudson observed that the exodus from Brahms Three had intensified. News of Goliath's proximity had obviously reached the scavenger town too, and as they set the Orion down and again exited into the container-lined streets, it was clear that the looting had gotten worse.

With weapons raised, Hudson led Tory through the narrow avenues towards the Landing Strip. Fights were breaking out all over, as looters clashed with store and home owners who were either unable to leave, or stubbornly didn't want to. Hudson knew the streets well enough to reach the Landing Strip while avoiding the worst hot spots. Bar a couple of brief scuffles – which ended as soon as the looters spotted Tory's Winchester rifle – they had made swift progress.

"We can cut through this side street then take a right," said Hudson, glancing around the corner. "Then we're pretty much there."

Tory nodded then returned to watching their backs, while Hudson crept ahead. Suddenly, a hand reached out from a dark doorway and grabbed his shoulder. He cursed himself for carelessly missing the alcove, and spun around to confront his attacker. Then he froze as the face of an attractive, young woman stared back at him. She looked vaguely familiar, Hudson thought, and she also looked distinctly pissed off.

"Oi, you rat bastard, you double-crossed me!" the street walker yelled at him. Tory arrived just in time to catch the woman slapping Hudson around the face. "You did a runner without paying what you promised me!"

Hudson rubbed his stinging cheek, though the sharp pain had also served to jolt his memory. It was the same street walker who he'd burst in on while she was 'entertaining' Private Hanes. With her help, he'd then stolen Hanes' uniform to gain entry to the CET Presidio so he could raid the vault. This was how he had first come to be in possession of the crystal, and Ericka's leather jacket, which he still wore. Hudson remembered that he'd promised to share the profits of the theft with the woman, in order to gain her cooperation. Then he had promptly left Brahms Three without doing so.

"Well, cough up what you owe then, you shithead!" the woman screeched at him.

Hudson shrugged and rapidly backed away, "Sorry, I didn't manage to get anything – that's why I'm still stuck here, like you."

The woman hurled a barrage of insults and curses at Hudson, before shouting, "I knew you were a shit robber!" and slamming the door.

Hudson let his breath out slowly, then realized that Tory was glowering at him.

"So, you ran out on a street walker without paying, huh?" said Tory folding her arms while still holding onto the Winchester, threateningly. "This had better be good..." she added, before raising her eyebrows and waiting expectantly for Hudson's explanation.

A couple of gunshots popped off down an adjacent street. Then another group of looters ran past, chased by a second gaggle wielding clubs and knives.

"Really, you're choosing now to ask about this?" said Hudson, echoing what Tory had said to him outside the massage parlor in the Gale Basin.

Suddenly, a looter stopped in the street and aimed a pistol at them. "Drop the fancy gun, lady! That's mine now!" he shouted.

Tory continued to lock eyes with Hudson, before casually swapping the Winchester to her left hand. She then drew her six-shooter, cocked it and pulled the trigger in less time than it had taken Hudson to breathe in and out. The looter fell, screaming and clutching his leg.

"Fine, but you'd better have a damn good explanation," Tory continued, while holstering the six-shooter again, as if nothing unusual had just happened. Hudson was speechless. "Now, before any more jilted street walkers slap you, where's this bar?"

Hudson pointed to the next side-street along, and Tory stormed away. The injured looter was trying to reach for his weapon, but Tory booted him in the head as she passed, knocking him out cold.

"Seems like you've got your own problems," came the voice of the street walker. She had popped her head back out of the door to see what the commotion was about. "Good!" she yelled, and slammed it shut again.

Hudson sucked in another deep breath to calm his already frayed nerves. Even with the prospect of Goliath arriving in the system at any moment, the one thing he feared more than anything was a vengeful Tory Bellona. He ran ahead and finally spotted the Landing Strip across the next street. Some of the windows had been smashed, and Hudson could clearly see that the door had been kicked in.

"We might already be too late," said Tory, as Hudson arrived at her side. She was reloading the Winchester and six-shooter in preparation for whatever might be waiting for them behind the door. "We go in hard," Tory added, her expression grave, "but be prepared; you might not like what we find in there."

"I understand," said Hudson. He appreciated Tory's frank warning, but he was still determined to discover Ma's fate. "Let's go."

Hudson covered Tory as they moved up to the door of the Landing Strip. Then Tory counted down from three on her fingers, before rushing inside, weapon raised. Hudson followed and immediately saw Ma on her knees in the middle of the floor, with her hands on her head. Standing behind her, with a pistol pressed to the back of her skull, was Rex Kove.

"Unless you want me to redecorate this place with your friend's brains, I'd put those guns down," said Rex. One of his two sons was emptying the till, while the other was in the back room, filling a bag with whatever he could find of value.

Hudson looked at Ma. She'd taken a bullet to the arm, and her face was bloodied too. Clearly, she hadn't given in without a fight. "Let her go, Rex," he called over. "Keep what you want, but just let her go."

"Like hell he can keep my stuff!" shouted Ma, but Rex just reached down and squeezed her wound, causing Ma to scream in agony.

"It's funny what you find out when you do some digging around," said Rex, smiling at Hudson. "Nice little setup you had going here; stashing some of your score for a rainy day." Rex's two sons were now also aiming their weapons at Hudson and Tory, in a sort of Mexican standoff. "So, I'm going to take what you owe me, and some more as interest," Rex continued. "And if you try to stop me, I kill the barkeep here. Then I'll kill you and your nutjob girlfriend too."

Hudson looked at Ma, and though she was in pain, he could see her mind was still sharp. They could try to shoot it out, he thought, but at such close range, even Tory wouldn't be able to get all three members of the gang, without getting hit too.

Hudson lowered his weapon, "Fine, just take what you want," he said, before turning to Tory, "It'll all be gone soon anyway."

Tory seemed to understand Hudson's meaning. There was no point dying to protect a bunch of things that were likely to be annihilated, along with the planet, in a matter of hours.

"Smart choice," said Rex. Then to his sons, he added. "Get their weapons."

Nervously, Rex's two sons moved out from behind the bar area, and approached Tory and Hudson. One of them tentatively reached for the 1873 Winchester, but Tory pulled it away from his grasping fingers.

"Touch this and I'll shove a barstool so far up your ass, I could use your head to sit down on," said Tory, locking eyes with the young man.

"Now, now, Tory," said Rex. "Let's not have any violence."

Suddenly, Ma spoke up, "You know what, violence sounds like a great idea..." she said, and thrust her head back into Rex's groin and abdomen. The burly hunter yelped and bent double, as Ma sprang up and tried to grapple the weapon from his hand.

Hudson used the distraction to land a hard-right cross to Rex's first son, before grabbing his scruffy brown hair and smashing his face into a table. Tory had also reacted quickly, stunning the other son with a couple of hard shots, before tossing him through a pile of stacked up chairs, like a bowling ball toppling nine pins. Hudson then ran to help Ma, but Rex had won their tussle and was again standing over her. One of his powerful hands was clenched over Ma's wounded shoulder, squeezing blood from it like water from a sponge. The other held a pistol to her head.

"Enough!" Rex yelled, "You had your warning, and now she pays the..."

A shot rang out, and Rex slumped to the floor, cracking his head on the bar on the way down. Hudson jerked around to see Tory lowering her six-shooter, smoke oozing from its barrel. His first thought was that Tory had killed Rex, but as he looked over, he saw that the muscular hunter was dazed, but still conscious. There was a single bullet wound to his left shoulder. Tory, remarkably, had shown him mercy.

Hudson rushed to Ma's side, and helped her to stand. Despite being beaten and shot up, she was as tough as ever.

"I'd have put that bullet in the asshole's head," said Ma, as she began to collect up the three hunters' weapons from the solid wood floor.

"I don't do that anymore," said Tory, holstering the antique revolver. "But I don't let bastards like Rex get away with doing it either."

"Fair enough," said Ma, as she tossed the hunters' weapons in the trash. She then grabbed a clean towel from behind the bar and tied it around her wounded arm.

One of Rex's sons recovered, and saw his father lying on the floor. He ran over to the man and dropped to his knees, yelling, "You've killed him!"

"I only wounded him," Tory corrected the young hunter, sounding a little annoyed at the accusation. "Don't make me regret it."

Ma turned to Hudson and said, "Grab the medical kit from behind the bar. I guess we can at least stop this lowlife from bleeding to death on my floor, not that he deserves it."

Hudson rushed around the other side of the counter and started searching for the kit. "Let the kid patch him up; we have to leave," he said, as he rummaged through the lower shelves. Then he found the medical kit and pulled it away from its mounting. It was caked in a thick coating of dust, and clearly hadn't been used for years, if ever.

"Leave?" replied Ma, incredulously. "I'm not going anywhere."

Hudson returned and placed the medical kit on the counter top. "Ma, Brahms Three is directly in that alien ship's path. It will literally tear the planet apart when it gets here."

Ma sighed and reached over the bar, grabbing a bottle of whiskey, though it wasn't one of her own. She pulled the cork out with her teeth and took a long swig, before her nose and eyes scrunched up.

"Hell, this crap is terrible," she said, tossing the bottle in the trash with the hunters' weapons.

"Ma, I'm serious, we have to go," repeated Hudson. "That's why we're here."

"It's good of you to check on me, Hudson, you always were a good kid," replied Ma, warmly. "But there's no telling if that ship will come here. It may just fly on past. Until I see it with my own eyes, I'm staying put."

The floor of the bar then began to shudder, as if a large ground transport had just rumbled past. Except that instead of the rumble fading as the transport moved further away, the vibration remained.

Hudson glanced over to Tory, and he could tell that the same thought had invaded her mind too. They both raced out of the Landing Strip and peered up, hoping that the massive shape of Goliath wasn't already looming above them. All of the looters had stopped too, and there now wasn't a single person on the street whose eyes weren't cast skyward. And they were all looking in the same direction. Hudson knew what had grabbed their attention, even before his own eyes saw it. Goliath had arrived, and it was coming straight for them.

Ma ran outside and looked up. For a few seconds, none of them spoke, before Ma simply said, "I don't believe it."

"Believe it," said Hudson. "This planet will be destroyed. I've already seen it destroy others."

Ma shook her head, "All that time hunting inside the alien wrecks, and I never once asked what took those brutes down to begin with." Then she looked at Hudson, and added, "You've seen this thing destroy entire planets?" Hudson nodded, and Ma shook her head again, and sighed. "I take it you've got your fancy ship here with you?"

"It's in the private dock you sorted for me," replied Hudson, still looking up at Goliath. As terrifying as it was to see, the great ship was also an awe-inspiring sight.

"Give me a couple of minutes," said Ma, before disappearing back inside the Landing Strip.

Hudson scowled, "Give you a couple of minutes? Ma, we have to go, now!" He ran inside after her and saw the ex-hunter carrying out the large bag of valuables that Rex's son had filled. She handed the bag to Hudson. "Anything else, or can we run away from the giant killer space ship now?" said Hudson, amazed at how coolly Ma was handling everything.

"Just one more thing," said Ma, rushing back behind the bar.

Hudson shook his head, and saw that both of Rex's sons were now kneeling at their father's side. Rex was still dazed, but coming around. Hudson ran up to the closest of the two sons, and the young man raised his guard. Hudson grabbed the medical kit off the table, and thrust it at him. "Patch him up, quickly. Then get the hell off this planet, while you still can."

He left the young man looking terrified and puzzled, and turned back to see Ma returning from behind the bar. She had a square bottle of her own-brand whiskey in each hand.

"Now, I'm ready to go," she said, nodding towards the door. "If I'm going to have to watch this planet die, I need a proper drink to send it off with."

CHAPTER 13

The few ships that were still left in Brahms Three's spaceport were blasting off without any regard for one another. Before Hudson, Tory and Ma had even reached the Orion, Hudson had seen two shuttles collide in mid-air and crash into the shipping-container city. However, as shocking as this was, he knew it soon wouldn't matter. The ground was starting to shake more violently, and Hudson realized that Brahms Three was on the verge of collapse.

Hudson had run ahead to get the Orion started, while Tory helped the injured Ma inside. He'd barely had time to drop into the pilot's seat, before he saw the arrow-like shape of seed ships soaring overhead. One cut through a departing freighter, smashing it apart like a walnut being cracked open.

"Martina is strapped in, go!" cried Tory as she dropped into the second seat and hurriedly fastened her harness.

Hudson lifted the Orion off the deck and pushed the throttle forward. Another freighter surged ahead of him and he threw the controls hard to port to avoid it, before a seed ship cut past and sliced a chunk out of the freighter's rear quarter. The larger ship's engines flashed out and it sank like a stone, before smashing through the control tower. It exploded like a bomb had just gone off, engulfing two other ships, before they could escape the inferno.

"We have a seed ship on our tail," Tory called out, as she activated the Orion's enhanced weapons systems. "If we stay in the atmosphere, it might level the playing field. We've seen how those things seem to defy physics."

"There won't be an atmosphere soon," Hudson replied. "Hell, there won't even be a planet in a few minutes, but I'll see what I can do..."

Hudson leveled off and pushed the Orion harder across the barren terrain of Brahms Three. The navigation scanner showed the seed ship in pursuit, but then a second chevron appeared close behind it. "Shit, there's two after us now!" Hudson called out, pushing the Orion as hard as he could. "I'll try to lose them."

Tory shook her head, "They're gaining too quickly, we have to destroy them, before they smash us like an egg."

Hudson checked the scanner again and saw that Tory was right. He tightened his grip on the throttle and steeled himself. "Hang on everyone!" he called out, hoping his voice would carry to Ma too. "Let's see if these alien bastards can handle a good, old-fashioned dogfight."

Hudson cut the throttle and hit the airbrakes, then pulled up. The g-forces pressed him hard against his harness, but he held the move until the two seed ships raced past. Pushing the throttle forwards again, he turned towards the nearest seed ship, which was banking hard to reacquire them.

"Take the shot!" cried Hudson, struggling to match the seed ship's sharp turning circle.

Energy bolts flashed out ahead of the Orion as Tory engaged the alien vessel. The first four bolts shot past the seed ship, narrowly missing, but then the next two landed square on the hull. The seed ship exploded and spiraled to the ground in flames.

Breathing out and sucking in another breath, Hudson craned his neck, looking for the second ship, before he saw it coming at them on a collision course. He throttled up and jinked the Orion in the opposite direction, and the seed ship shot past, missing only by meters. Hudson wrestled to regain control as the pressure wave buffeted the Orion, then he turned towards the seed ship, which was trying to loop around to make another run.

Hudson watched anxiously as the targeting reticule searched for a lock. *Come on!* Hudson urged, as the seed ship completed its turn and accelerated towards them. Then the crosshairs locked on and Tory fired. Without waiting to find out if she'd hit, Hudson banked hard, then the burning remains of the seed ship roared past, like a giant flaming arrow.

"That was close!" Tory called out, as Hudson pulled the Orion into a steep climb.

"Too close!" Hudson shouted back, peering out of the window at the surface of the planet, which was now breaking apart. "But we're not out of this yet," Hudson added, switching the waypoint on the navigation scanner to the portal's location.

The Orion surged through the remains of the planet's collapsing atmosphere and into space, directly into the path of the core matter that Goliath had ejected. It was glowing, like a mini sun, bleeding its heat into space. Hudson knew that it would soon fall into the planet's gravity well and turn Brahms Three into the galaxy's latest asteroid field.

Hudson veered away from the core matter and accelerated the ship towards the portal, before quickly glancing down at the navigation scanner again. No other seed ships were in pursuit; they were in the clear. Hudson allowed his muscles to relax and then throttled back, before spinning the ship around to take one final look at Brahms Three.

"What the hell kind of power can do that?" said Ma, suddenly appearing at Hudson's side. The planet was already fractured and collapsing into itself.

Hudson glanced up at Ma. He'd never seen her looking so sullen. It was like the breaking apart of the planet had fractured her heart too. He brought up an enlarged view of Goliath on one of the monitors. The great ship was still turned towards the planet, as if gleefully spectating its demise.

"That's what can do this," said Hudson. The sight of Goliath still sent a chill down his spine.

Ma sighed heavily, then simply said, "Why?"

Hudson wasn't used to hearing sadness in Ma's voice. Even on a planet that was as bleak as Brahms Three could often be, she had always maintained a sunny disposition. However, faced with Goliath's apocalyptic power, she was reduced to asking the one simple question that mattered.

"Hate," replied Hudson, solemnly. "Nothing more. That ship is a raw nerve. It's pure rage, and all it wants to do is destroy us."

Hudson heard the material covering his headrest creak as Ma tightened her grip on it. It was like she was imagining she could somehow choke the life out of the alien that had destroyed her home.

"So, how do we kill it?" Ma asked, before meeting Hudson's eyes. "There must be a way to kill it, right?"

Hudson looked back at what remained of Brahms Three, then at the image of Goliath, which was slowly turning towards the portal, and gathering up its seed ships, ready to unleash them again on its next victim. He gave a slight shrug. "I hope so."

Ma moved away for a second, then returned with a square bottle of whiskey. She removed the cork and said, "To Brahms Three. And to taking out the alien bastard that destroyed it." She took a swig, before handing the bottle to Hudson. He drank and then passed it to Tory, who did the same, also without saying a word. Then they watched in silence, as Brahms Three was finally reduced to rock and dust.

CHAPTER 14

Griff stepped off the dilapidated shuttle that Yaeger had sold them on Mars and looked around the rendezvous point. Despite being a popular tourist spot, Cutler Wendell had chosen an area of Point Reyes that was well off the beaten track. This, combined with the fact most people on Earth seemed to be hunkered down in fear of the approaching alien invader, meant there was no-one else around for at least a kilometer in any direction. However, there was also no sign of the hostile mercenary, either.

The roar of another ship's engines filled the air and Griff watched as Jane Wash circled around in her personal RGF Transport, before landing a couple of hundred meters away. Her transport was basically a standard RGF Patrol Craft, but without the weapons and with considerably more creature comforts. It was a perk of Wash's former position that she obviously hadn't wanted to give up. Certainly, compared to the crappy shuttle that Cutler had traded his desirable FS-31 for, it was luxurious. Wash's ship also worked faultlessly, which was something that also could not be said for the shuttle. This was despite Swinsler's inept attempts to rush through some rapid repairs. If it hadn't been for the shuttle's hazardous condition, he would have taken great pleasure in suggesting that Cutler trade the crystal for Wash's ship instead. He was still considering it, just to see the look on the cantankerous witch's face, but as much as it would bring him satisfaction, his own sense of self-preservation had prevailed.

"So, where is he?" asked Wash, promenading up beside Griff and hugging herself tightly as a gentle breeze picked up. Griff had never seen anyone look so ill-at-ease in the outdoors as Wash looked then. Boardrooms and social engagements were her natural habitat; anywhere that she could brown-nose other members of the military and political elite.

"How the hell should I know?" snapped Griff. "I'm sure he's lurking around here somewhere."

Wash drew her pistol and moved closer to Griff, almost as though she was using him as a shield.

Griff shook his head, "Relax, he's not going to shoot us, at least not until he has the shuttle," he said. "I have to transfer the ID fob to him first, otherwise he won't be able to fly it. I can't do that if I'm already dead."

Wash didn't seem convinced, "But he flew it back here from Mars, surely he already has the same access you do?"

Griff held up the fob, "I already used the RGF bypass hardware to delete his ID. I'm not stupid."

Wash raised her eyebrows, "That is debatable." Griff glared back then turned away to resume his survey of the surrounding area. "Well, I guess we'd better hope that Cutler has a higher opinion of me than you do," he answered, testily.

"Again, I doubt it," sneered Wash.

Griff was a second away from spinning around and throttling his former commander, but then he caught sight of something moving out of the trees. Moments later, Cutler Wendell appeared, walking out into the open brazenly and seemingly without fear.

"There he is," said Griff, pointing Cutler out to Wash. He noted that the mercenary didn't appear to be armed, and that his shoulder was also heavily strapped up, but from the quality of the work, it didn't look to have been self-administered. Griff became immediately suspicious, and drew his sidearm just to be sure, but held it low.

"I am unarmed," said Cutler in his droning voice. "So, you can holster your weapons."

"Like I'm going to trust you, after the shit you pulled?" laughed Griff. "You're lucky I don't just shoot you now, and take the crystal off your still warm body."

Cutler did not appear at all intimidated by Griff's warning. "I suspected you might threaten such an obvious act," said the mercenary, contemptuously, "which is naturally why the crystal is inside a locked container. A real lock, not one that your infamous RGF skeleton keys would be able to open."

"Yeah, well I also erased your ID from the shuttle's fob, before you get any ideas about stealing it," Griff hit back, eager to show he was just as shrewd as Cutler.

Seemingly emboldened by Cutler's lack of a weapon, Wash stepped forward. "Can you two blowhards just skip the foreplay so we can get down to business?" she said, straightening her back, and looking down her nose at Cutler. "Do you have the crystal or not?"

Cutler slowly reached into his jacket pocket, watched attentively by Griff and Wash, then removed a small metal box. "I merely want the shuttle," he said. "Then I will gladly depart, and you will never see me again."

Griff was still suspicious; it all seemed to be too easy, and also too reasonable. He had expected Cutler to push for more than a crapped-out old shuttlecraft. He pointed to Cutler's shoulder, "You seem to have been patched up pretty well. Who helped you?"

Cutler smiled, "Ah, the ever-paranoid Logan Griff," he said, in a flat, mocking tone. "It may shock you to know that, unlike yourself, I do have other acquaintances on Earth."

"Just no-one who would buy the crystal from you?" replied Griff, still pushing. There was something about Cutler's demeanor he found off, before he then realized what it was – the mercenary wasn't angry. Even for someone as generally composed as Cutler was, he still expected a great deal of bitterness and resentment over what had happened.

"As I'm sure you are aware, this crystal is wanted by the CET and MP, which makes it a somewhat difficult item to move," replied Cutler. "For you two distinguished RGF officers, however, it may provide enough leverage to keep you out of a cell. For me, a mere mercenary, it would not."

Wash holstered her weapon, and stepped forward. "Okay, let's just get this done, so I can get out of these damn woods," she snapped. She started vigorously rubbing her shoulders, as if she were standing at the South Pole, rather than the breezy, but moderate climate of the national seashore. "Open the box, and put it on the ground, then back away. Griff will set the ID fob to imprint mode, and toss it to you when we have the item."

Cutler shook his head, "I am not opening this box while you two are still armed," he said, smoothly. He looked over to his left, "Toss your weapons into the long grass, then we can make the exchange."

Griff was about to tell Cutler where he could get off, but Wash cut in.

"Fine, if that will satisfy you," she said, before tossing her weapon. Then she looked at Griff, expectantly.

"Are you mad?" he hissed.

"Just toss the damn pistol," Wash snapped. "If he tries anything, it's two on one, and he's injured." Then she looked at Griff, provokingly, "Even someone as puny and pitiable as you should be able to subdue an injured man."

Griff growled, then tossed his weapon too. "There, now open the damn box and piss off," he snapped, pulling a cigarette from his breast pocket.

Cutler smiled, before entering the combination into the lock and opening the lid. He set the box down, so that Griff and Wash could clearly see the contents, and took two paces back. "Now, the ID fob, if you don't mind," he said, opening a hand towards Griff.

Griff lit the cigarette and held the shuttle's ID fob in front of his face. He activated it and said, "Voice print ID, Logan Griff. Erase and set imprint mode." The fob bleeped, scanned his eyes, then flashed green. Griff sucked on the cigarette, and tossed Cutler the device.

"A pleasure," said Cutler, catching the ID fob with one hand, and backing away towards the shuttle. He was still wearing a saccharin smile, which continued to make Griff feel anxious.

Wash collected the box and plucked out the crystal, before discarding the container like a piece of trash. "Is this it?" she asked, holding the crystal up to the light and sounding hugely unimpressed. "I expected something more ornate."

"It's not a piece of damn costume jewelry," grumbled Griff, turning to look at Wash. Then he saw the crystal in her hand and snatched it from her. "Shit!" he cursed, before turning back to Cutler. "This isn't it! That double-crossing bastard has conned us!"

Wash screamed, then ran to find her weapon. "Don't just stand there, go after him!" she yelled, as she frantically scrambled around in the long grass.

Griff shoved the fake crystal into his pocket and raced after the mercenary. Then he saw more movement in the trees ahead, and abruptly stopped, skidding across the dry grass. Cutler was already at the shuttle, but before he went inside, he turned back to face Griff. He was smiling more broadly than ever.

"I was not lying when I said the crystal didn't provide me sufficient leverage," Cutler shouted out to Griff. "But handing you and Miss Wash over to the CET authorities gave me all the leverage I needed."

"You bastard, I'll get you for this!" Griff roared. Then he heard urgent shouts from the trees ahead, and saw the distinctive uniforms of CET soldiers advancing.

Griff turned and ran back towards Wash's RGF Transport. "It's a trap!" he shouted, as Wash came towards him, weapon in hand. She glanced over towards the shuttle and saw the CET soldiers. Instinctively, she fired four shots towards them, forcing the soldiers to dive behind cover, and then ran after Griff.

Shouts of "freeze" and "stand down" blared out behind, but Griff ignored them. He reached the RGF Transport and searched for another weapon. Finding a flare gun, Griff leaned around the door and shot at the approaching soldiers, hitting one in the chest with the burning projectile. The soldier went down, screaming, in a cloud of bright red smoke. Wash raced inside, slapping her pistol into Griff's hand, before running to the cockpit.

"Keep firing at them!" she yelled, as she powered up the engines, bypassing all the safety checks.

Griff continued to shoot until he emptied his magazine. The RGF Transport suddenly lifted off, and Griff had to grab hold of the handle on the inside of the door to keep from falling out. Gunfire crackled at them from below, and bullets pinged off the hull of the transport, but, like the RGF Patrol Crafts, the ship was hardened and designed to take enemy fire.

Griff hauled himself back inside and hit a button to close the hatch. He then dragged himself into the cockpit, as Wash turned south along the shoreline, staying as low as possible.

"Head North!" yelled Griff, realizing that Wash seemed to be flying back towards San Francisco.

"No, we need to reach the city," Wash shouted back. "They won't attack us over a populated area."

Griff shook his head, and climbed into the second seat. "Damn it, Wash, what kind of bubble do you pen-pushers live in?" he snapped, "The city's air defenses will destroy us before any CET patrol can! Head towards Canada, we have to lose them in the forests!"

Wash turned out over the water and then back north, remarkably without any complaint or curt response. Griff fastened his harness and checked the navigation scanner, but already he could see two red CET blips approaching.

"I'll kill that rat bastard, I swear I will!" Griff yelled, slamming his fists onto the armrests and cursing himself for not seeing Cutler's deception sooner. "That's the last time Cutler Wendel gets the better of me."

Yet, despite his angry declarations, Griff knew that Cutler Wendell was now the least of his problems. All that mattered was avoiding capture, and in order to succeed, he was once again forced to rely on the most unlikely of allies.

CHAPTER 15

Griff anxiously tracked the progress of the pursuing CET ships on the scanner, as Wash continued to fly fast and low up the northern coast of California. The two CET vessels were still in pursuit, but there were also multiple new warnings on his monitor. The whole state had been put on alert, and he knew they wouldn't be able to stay airborne for long.

"In a few minutes, there will be a half-dozen ships closing in on us; we can't outrun them all," Griff called over to Wash. He'd always considered his old boss to be a narcissistic bureaucrat whose only skill was self-advancement, but she was handling the transport with surprising proficiency. "We should think about leaving the planet, and making a run for a portal."

Wash briefly glanced at the navigation scanner, then shook her head. "We won't make it, not with most of the CET fleet already in orbit."

The communications panel lit up and Griff saw that there was an incoming message from the pursuing CET ships. He opened a channel and put it through.

"RGF Transport, we have been ordered to escort you to CET Base Travis," came the authoritative voice of the CET patrol pilot. "Fail to comply with this order and you will be fired upon. Please respond."

Griff noticed that the CET patrol craft had also transmitted a flight plan. He glanced over to Wash, and said, "If we land at Travis then it's over for us, but we have to respond with something." He then watched her, trying to gauge her reaction, but Wash remained impassive. "Wash, what the hell? We need to answer them!" he shouted, losing his patience with her.

"I'm thinking, damn it," snapped Wash. Then she quickly glanced at the navigation scanner again, before throttling back and grabbing her headset. "CET Patrol Craft, message received. Proceeding to CET Base Travis."

"What? Did you not just hear what I said?" snapped Griff, as Wash threw down the headset, and began to follow the new course they had received.

"How the hell could I not hear you?" barked Wash, "You should grow that ridiculous fur on your top lip a bit thicker, so that maybe it will muffle the sound of your bothersome voice."

Griff threw his hands out wide, "So, what? You're giving up, is that your genius plan?"

"Of course not, you idiot!" snarled Wash. "There's an RGF training base up near Sonoma. The flight plan they gave us takes us right past it. When we get close enough, I'll divert and land us there."

Griff thought for a moment. He was aware of the training base up on the Sonoma Mountain. It was certainly big enough that they might be able to blend in and slip away unseen. However, there was still a problem with Wash's improvised plan. "How can you be sure they'll let us land?" asked Griff. "The CET authorities have taken control of the RGF, remember?"

Wash shook her head, "I can't be sure, but do you have any better ideas?"

Griff rubbed his temples, wracking his brains to think of an alternative, but nothing came to mind. "Shit, it's worth a shot," he said, wearily. Then he had an idea, "Hey, do you know anyone stationed at the training base? Someone we could maybe claim to be?"

Wash's brow furrowed in concentration, as Griff noticed one of the CET patrols pull in line with them off their starboard side. He could see the pilot through the cockpit glass, glancing over at him, suspiciously.

"I think Superintendent Farlow still runs the station," answered Wash. "You could try him; his voice is almost as annoying as yours is."

"Cute..." replied Griff, scowling back at her. He then pulled his console closer and locked in the frequency for the control tower at Sonoma Mountain RGF Training Base. He scrambled the channel then turned to Wash, "Ready when you are," he added, while pulling on his headset.

Griff and Wash both watched the navigation scanner closely, as they began to climb over the mountain. Then he saw Wash grab hold of the throttle control and glance over to him.

"Make the call," she ordered, before slamming the throttle forward and veering sharply towards the base.

Griff was pressed back into his seat from the sudden acceleration, and his hand slipped away from his console.

"Griff, now!" shouted Wash, as the training base came into view ahead.

"A little warning next time!" Griff cursed, while pushing himself upright and opening the channel. "Sonoma Mountain, this is Superintendent Farlow, requesting an emergency landing," he blurted into the mic. He'd intended to make his voice sound urgent, but the fact he was genuinely panicking meant there was no need to act.

Griff waited, but there was silence. "Sonoma Mountain, I am declaring an emergency, do you read?!" he cried out.

Then the radio crackled on, and an anxious voice replied. "RGF Transport, this is Sonoma Mountain RGF Training Base. Who did you say you were again?"

Griff shook his head. It was just his luck to find the most incompetent tower operator in the whole of RGF. "Superintendent Farlow, damn it!" he yelled. "Requesting an emergency landing."

There was another painful silence, during which time Wash and Griff exchanged nervous glances. Then the radio crackled back on, but this time it was a different, far more assured voice.

"Who is this? Identify yourself?"

Griff couldn't believe it. "For the third time, I am Superintendent Farlow! Don't they teach you dumb rooks anything!"

There was another pause, this time much shorter, before the voice replied. "I am Superintendent Ray Farlow."

Griff threw his head back, and then looked at Wash. Her expression was the same as his. They both knew they were sunk. Suddenly warning alarms sounded in the cockpit, as weapons locked onto them from the RGF base, but before they had a chance to fire, the transport was hit from the rear. More alarms sounded, and Griff closed his eyes, as the ship began to rapidly lose altitude.

"We've been hit!" Wash shouted, her voice desperate and panicky, but Griff ignored her cries. "Griff!" he heard Wash yell again, but he just kept his eyes closed, and concentrated on the drone of the alarm. "Griff, do something! Griff!"

Then the cockpit glass shattered and Logan Griff was jolted forward against his harness as the RGF Transport plummeted into the mountainside.

CHAPTER 16

Logan Griff had flown millions of kilometers during his RGF career, not even counting the vast distances between portal transitions. Yet, that had been the first time he had crashed. It wasn't an experience he ever wanted to repeat.

Whether out of luck or judgement, the CET Patrol Craft had delivered just enough damage to bring them down, but not enough to destroy them outright. It was possible that Wash's better-than-expected piloting skills had also contributed to their survival, though Griff would never have admitted that to her. However, since his eyes had been shut for the crash, he didn't know whether they had been saved by Wash's crash-landing expertise, or pure, dumb luck.

Their close proximity to the RGF training base had also contributed to their narrow escape. Fire Transports had arrived on the scene swiftly and pulled Griff and Wash from the burning wreckage. Medics had quickly treated the cuts, bruises and minor burns that both he and Wash had suffered, before CET security had placed them under arrest. Now, as he lay on the rock-hard bed in the cell inside the Sonoma Mountain RGF base, with Jane Wash shrieking at the guards to let her out, he contemplated whether his survival had been a blessing or a curse.

"Can you shut the hell up for two damn seconds?!" Griff shouted over to Wash, as she bellowed yet another barrage of orders at a passing guard. "They're not going to let you out." Then he sat up and looked Wash in the eyes. "Don't you get it yet? You're no longer 'Superintendent' Wash; you're just plain old Jane Wash. You're nothing to them."

"We'll see about that," Wash spat back. Then she jabbed a finger into her own sternum. "I'm still connected. I know people. And when this whole shit storm is over, they'll take me back." Wash then raised her voice, and directed it towards the two cell guards, "Then all of these assholes who refused to help me now will pay the price!"

Griff rubbed his eyes and shook his head. "You're deluding yourself," he replied, lying back down on the bed. "All of your 'connections' are in cells just like this one. You're on your own."

It was in sticky situations like this that Griff would normally have turned to Wash to bail him out. Now he had to think of another solution, but with Wash's incessant, high-pitched yammering, he couldn't concentrate for more than a few seconds.

Suddenly the door to the cell block opened and a late middle-aged man wearing a CET officer's uniform walked in, accompanied by two armed CET soldiers. Griff stood up, recognizing the man by his rank, if not by his face. He'd never met Commodore Trent before, but everyone in the RGF knew him by reputation. Griff glanced across to Wash, and it was apparent from the look on her face that she'd recognized him too.

"It's about time someone with authority showed up," said Wash, storming over to where Trent now waited. "I demand to be released from this cell, Commodore. You have no right to hold me!"

Trent's eyebrows raised up on his forehead, then he casually pressed his hands behind his back. "Actually, your breaches of aviation regulations are more than enough on their own to merit me holding you," Trent replied, smoothly. "But shooting at CET soldiers, not to mention your breach of the Relic Guardian Force contract, largely overshadows such trivialities."

Griff winced, and stole a sideways glance at Wash. His former commander was used to people fearing her, and jumping to attention when she spoke their names. The fact that Trent was clearly not intimidated by Wash would only piss her off even more.

Wash straightened her back, practically squaring off against the Commodore, despite the thick steel bars separating them. "How was I to know that your soldiers were not other mercenaries, hired by the criminal outlaw, Cutler Wendell?" She jabbed a finger at Trent, "An outlaw that you colluded with, I might add." She tucked her hand back under her arm, and continued. "It is no surprise we ran for our lives. As for the incident at Chrome One, I am merely the fall guy for decisions made by my superiors."

Griff raised an eyebrow and looked back at Trent. Wash had delivered her speech with composure, but he doubted that her, 'I was only following orders' strategy to deflect blame onto her superiors would hold up for long.

Trent smiled and said, "That's interesting, because your superiors claim you acted alone." His manner was still polite, but his tone was a touch sharper now. "But it matters not; you shall all share the same fate. Either way, now that I am in command of this base, rather than your wretched former organization, you shall remain here, as my guests." Then Trent removed the crystal fragment from his pocket and held it up. "I have what I need from you already."

Griff laughed, drawing an even more scornful look from Trent. "Do you find it amusing that planets are being destroyed? Does it entertain you that millions have already died, and billions more are under threat?" asked Trent, though it was a rhetorical question. "This crystal could be all that stands in the way of the alien invader. Yet you two horse-traded it like it was no more significant than a common CPU shard."

"You can't believe that alien vessel poses any real threat?" replied Wash, derisively. "Your entire space fleet, and that of the MP, stands in its way. It is only one vessel, no matter how big it is."

Trent sighed and shook his head. "I hope we all survive this, because I will enjoy seeing you tried and convicted for your crimes." He slipped the crystal back in his pocket. "And if not, you'll die along with the rest of us." Then he pointed to the hard cot bed in the corner of the cell, and added, "Enjoy your stay."

Trent began to walk away, but Griff was determined to have the last word. The CET Commodore may not have been as pompous as most, but his smug superiority and clear disdain for the Relic Guardian Force made Griff hate him all the same.

"It's a fake," Griff called over. Trent stopped, and wheeled around to face him, brow furrowed. "That's right, Cutler Wendell took you for a fool, Commodore. He gave you a cheap piece of tat, and you bought his lies, hook, line and sinker." Griff could see that he had embarrassed and angered the

Commodore, and smiled, before sitting down on the edge of his cot bed. "Not too smart after all, are we?"

Griff also saw Wash's eyes narrow and her lips curl into a spiteful sneer. Then the Commodore spun around again.

"Make sure they are guarded around the clock," he barked, breaking character from his usual charming self. Then he marched out of the door, and slammed it shut behind him.

"I enjoyed that," said Griff, after the sharp crack of the door slamming had cleared from his head. "Even if we are stuck here, at least that asshole got pushed out of his high tower."

Wash also sat down on the end of her bed. "We aren't stuck here," she said, casually, before glancing at Griff. "This isn't over yet."

CHAPTER 17

Griff woke with a start. A hand was pressed over his mouth, and a figure was standing above him, but in the darkness, he couldn't make out who it was. He let out a muffled cry, and struggled against the hand pressing down on his face, but panic was taking its hold. Then he saw the glint of something metal looming over his neck and he froze. *Cutler has found me!* he thought, before closing his eyes and waiting for the blade to sink into his flesh.

"Will you stop squirming around!" came the voice of Jane Wash. Even though the volume of her demand was muted, it lacked none of its customary spikiness.

Griff opened his eyes and saw that the glint had merely been moonlight reflecting off Wash's diamond earrings. His whole body went limp, but his heart was still pounding in his chest. The relief he felt was like waking from a recurring childhood nightmare.

Wash removed her hand from Griff's mouth and looked at it at in disgust, before wiping the saliva onto his black shirt.

"What the hell is the matter with you?" Wash continued, still keeping the volume of her snarls low.

Griff sat up and wiped his mouth with his sleeve, before hawking a globule of spit onto the stone floor. He could taste Wash's perfume on his lips and it repulsed him.

"What's the matter with *me*?" he hit back, though also keeping a lid on the volume of his protests. "What the hell are *you* doing waking me up like that? I thought Cutler had come to slit my throat in the night!"

"How was I to know you'd react like a frightened toddler?" Wash hit back. "You're lucky I didn't slit your throat myself – I was sorely tempted."

Griff looked around the cell. Moonlight shone through the solitary, letterbox window, and a single guard sat asleep at the desk by the door. "I take it you have a reason for getting me up in the middle of the night?" Griff asked, stretching his arms and shoulders. "Because you're missing out on your beauty sleep, and you really, really need it."

"Cute," said Wash, echoing something Griff had said to her previously. "But yes, I obviously have a reason. And since your lazy, useless ass isn't going to get us out of here, it's down to me."

Griff relaxed back against the wall and folded his arms. "You woke me up so that we could escape?" he replied, making his doubtfulness apparent in both his voice and body language.

"Believe me, I'd rather leave you here, but unfortunately I will still need your help," replied Wash. Then she held up a small, square object.

Griff frowned and leaned closer so that he could see it better in the gloom. He raised another doubtful eyebrow at Wash.

"You're telling me you've had a skelly on you all this time?" he asked, and Wash nodded. He wanted to slap the smug, shit-eating grin off her face, but the truth was, he was also impressed.

"Where the hell were you hiding that?" Griff continued, aware that they had both been searched before being put in the cell, which was how Trent had come to be in possession of the fake crystal. "It can't have been down your cleavage, since you don't have any. And your bony ass barely fills those skinny pants, so between your butt cheeks is out of the question too." Then he scowled, "Unless you had it stuck *up* your ass?"

Out of nowhere, Wash slapped him hard across the cheek. The sharp clap, set against the surrounding stillness of the cell, was like a glass smashing. Griff and Wash both glanced over to the guard, who snuffled softly, but continued sleeping.

"Watch your filthy mouth," snarled Wash, jabbing a finger at him, "and get your head out of the gutter and in the game. If we're going to break out of here, it will require some extreme measures. I need to be sure you're prepared to do what's necessary."

The sharp slap had fully woken up Griff's senses. It had also intensified his desire to murder Wash, slowly and painstakingly. He rubbed his cheek and answered, "Don't worry about me. You get that door open, and I'll do whatever needs to be done."

Wash's eyes narrowed. "Good, because now there are no half-measures."

Griff frowned. "I thought you were 'connected'?" he said, snarkily. "I thought your fancy lawyers and contacts were going to get you exonerated?"

Wash shook her head. "As much as it pains me to admit it, you were right," she replied. "Trent said so himself. The senior commanders will all hang, and they'll just string us up alongside them."

Wash's admission that he'd been right felt triumphant. He'd never seen Wash back down before, ever, but he still wanted to be sure that she fully understood what escape meant for both of them. Breaches of the Relic Guardian Force contract and air traffic violations were one thing, but a forced breakout of a holding cell was quite another. Especially if the cost came in lives.

"Just how far are you willing to go, Wash?" said Griff, wanting to make sure his former commander understood the stakes.

"I'll leave that up to you," replied Wash, before she skulked up to the cell door, watching to make sure the guard was still asleep. She then attached the skelly to the lock and activated it.

Griff crept up next to Wash and watched the lights on the little device flash wildly. "That waste of space over there could wake up before this thing breaks the lock," he complained, but Wash just shushed him.

"This is just a rookie training base," she replied. "These cells are used for nothing more exciting than the occasional drunken misdemeanor." Then the skelly blinked green and deactivated, before the lock clicked open. "Which means they don't bother to keep the lock codes up-to-date," she added, with another smug smile, before pocketing the skelly.

Griff cautiously pushed open the cell door. It squeaked softly, like a bicycle wheel in need of a squirt of oil. Griff winced and held his breath, all the while watching the guard for any signs he was stirring. Then he cautiously crept outside and approached the sleeping man. His ID keyfob was still attached to his belt, and his sidearm was also still holstered. However, he'd placed his nightstick on the table, along with some other bulkier items, presumably so he could get more comfortable for his regulation-breaking nap.

Picking up the nightstick, Griff crept around behind the guard, before grasping it in both hands. He met Wash's eyes, which were staring back at him inquisitively. He knew he could stun the guard, or incapacitate him in some other way, but if he woke and raised the alarm, they'd be recaptured and moved somewhere far more secure. That would end any hopes of escape, permanently. However, he also wanted to test Wash's resolve. He wanted to see how far the pen-pusher was really willing to go.

Maintaining eye contact with Wash, he hooked the nightstick around the guard's neck. Then, sucking in a breath and holding it, he pulled back hard, putting all of his strength and weight into the effort of choking the man.

Wash continued to watch, impassively, as the guard struggled and croaked and spluttered. But Griff did not relax his hold. The man's struggles soon grew weaker, and eventually stopped altogether. Griff finally released his hold on the nightstick, and breathed out, shaking his throbbing hands. His breathing was rapid and labored, as his lungs struggled to feed air to his oxygen-starved body. The guard, conversely, was no longer breathing at all.

Wash stepped forward, still watching Griff closely. Griff studied her expression and stance, hoping that his actions had shocked her in some way. If he couldn't have her respect, he wanted her to fear him; but Wash appeared unmoved.

"You could have just knocked him out," said Wash, while reaching down to remove the guard's weapon. She also took a spare magazine, which she placed into her pocket.

"No half-measures, remember?" replied Griff.

Wash's penetrating stare persisted for a second longer, then she loaded the sidearm, before adding, casually, "Make sure you get his ID fobs."

Griff wasn't sure whether to be annoyed or impressed with Wash's detached composure, but since he'd been foolish enough to allow Wash to take the guard's sidearm, he did as she asked. Keen to have some additional weapons at his disposal – as much to protect himself against Wash as against the other guards – he also removed the dead man's stun weapon and incapacitant spray. Neither was as good as the CET issue pistol, but it was better than nothing, he considered.

"Okay, genius, so what's the plan now?" said Griff. He'd guessed, or at least hoped, that Wash had thought further ahead than simply escaping the cell.

"The student officers have all been sent home, until this mess with the CET and RGF is ironed out," said Wash. "Which means the base has a skeleton crew." She walked over to the door and looked through the window, before turning back to Griff. "So, we walk out of here, commandeer a flyer, and figure out our next move."

Griff laughed, "We just 'walk out of here'? How do you propose pulling that off?"

Wash pointed to the dead guard. "You put on that uniform, and march me out of here as your prisoner."

Griff looked at the guard again. He must have been three inches shorter than Griff, and twenty pounds heavier. "I'll look like a damn idiot wearing that," he complained.

"What else is new?" replied Wash, acidly. "And I can hardly wear it, can I?" she added, gesturing to her own slender frame. "I'm five six and one hundred and ten pounds. It would look like I'm wearing a refuse sack."

"A sack would at least hide your bony ass," Griff hit back, still smarting from Wash's earlier snide remark. "But fine, I'll wear it." Then he sneered at Wash, remembering how she would regularly frequent the seedy establishments in the scavenger towns, and added, "So long as I get to cuff you. I know you like that kind of thing."

Wash stepped in and went to slap Griff again, but this time he caught her by the wrist. "Careful, Wash," he growled. "Be careful."

Wash stepped back and folded her arms, still holding the guard's firearm. Then she raised her eyebrows, and looked at the dead body again. "I'm waiting..."

Griff sighed and began to undress. *If Wash wants a peep show, I'll give her one*, he thought, while removing his shirt. "What is our next move, anyway?" he said, dumping the shirt on the desk. "Assuming we manage to just 'walk out of here' that is."

Wash's face had adopted a sort of impish smirk. Griff had always known about her various perversions, but even so, he wasn't sure whether she was just enjoying his humiliation, or genuinely enjoying watching him undress.

"By now that impudent bore, Commodore Trent, will have frozen our accounts and revoked our IDs," said Wash, her eyes flicking down as Griff lowered his pants. "So, there is really only one thing we can do."

"And what's that?" said Griff, throwing his pants at Wash in an attempt to stop her staring.

Wash caught the flying garment, but then her smile twisted into something more sinister. "We find Cutler Wendell..." she snarled. "He will think he's safe, but he is not. We find him, and we take everything he has." Then she met Griff's eyes, and all traces of her prior playfulness had gone. "And then we kill him."

CHAPTER 18

The swirling purple vortex finally snapped shut as the enormous frame of the Revocater emerged from the portal. Liberty turned the hulking vessel towards their next waypoint and immediately saw the fractured remains of a planet swing into view. It was now little more than a concentrated asteroid field of rock and ice.

"What planet was this?" Liberty asked, as the location of the next portal appeared on the screen ahead of her. She completed the turn and locked in the course, without thinking. Piloting the enormous Revocater had almost become second nature to her.

"That is the remains of the planet you called Aphrodite Four," came the disembodied voice of Morphus. The entity's female form then rose up out of the second seat, but remained physically embedded into it, as it had done before. "It was a member planet of the Union of Outer Portal Worlds," it continued. "However, Goliath has already extinguished all life on all of the worlds associated with this faction."

Liberty shook her head in disbelief. "All the OPW planets are already gone? But that's millions of people!" she asked, still struggling to believe it. "What about the CET and MP portal worlds?"

Morphus appeared lost in thought for a moment. It was still struggling to balance the management of the prototype Revocater's systems with its own functions.

"The latest data I intercepted from the seed drones is outdated," Morphus eventually replied. "But if Goliath remains unaware of our presence, it will eradicate the most distant CET and MP worlds first, before methodically working its way towards System 5118208."

Liberty frowned. "And what if it is already aware of our presence?"

Morphus' head turned to face Liberty, while remaining part of the seat. It was a peculiar thing to see, and a little unsettling too.

"If Goliath is aware of our return, then it will already be heading for Earth," said Morphus, with an almost human melancholy. Then its head snapped forward again and its expression became rigid, like a shop mannequin. "Stand by, I am detecting seed ships still in the system," Morphus added, more urgently. The display at the front of the replica cockpit then updated to show multiple formations of what looked like hundreds of the arrow-shaped vessels.

"What are they doing?" asked Liberty, watching as the ships seemed to be grouping more closely together into distinct clusters. "They look like they're going to collide with each other."

"Not collide," said Morphus. "Combine."

Liberty continued to watch as the different groups of seed ships began to attach to one another, like a giant 3D puzzle. The shape quickly began to grow, with more and more seed ships flying in, adding to the new object's mass. Then the image pulled back, and Liberty saw not one, but three of these new diamond-shaped objects coming towards them. They were still diminutive compared to the Revocater, but in sheer volume, they were twice the size of the bigger cruisers in the MP and CET armadas.

"What the hell are they?" asked Liberty, starting to feel her pulse quicken.

"The closest translation in your language would be infiltrators," replied Morphus. "Goliath has left them behind in case anything tried to pass through this system from the Corporeals' homeworld." Morphus again appeared to be lost in thought, as some other aspect of the Revocater demanded its fuller attention. "It may yet be unaware that I have located another Revocater," Morphus resumed a few seconds later, "but at the very least, the great ship suspects something is wrong."

Liberty sucked in a long breath and grabbed the controls. "What do I do?"

Morphus sank back into the seat, like butter soaking into hot toast. "You must accelerate your progress to the portal," replied Morphus, its voice again an ethereal presence in the chamber. "The infiltrators may only be a fraction of our size, but three of them together still possess the capability to damage this vessel."

Liberty regained control of the ship and pushed the throttle forward, but the infiltrators had already positioned themselves between the Revocater and the portal. "Can you destroy them first?" she asked, hoping that was why Morphus had sunk away.

"I will try," said Morphus, but its voice sounded tired and unconvincing.

Liberty concentrated on the infiltrators, and the image ahead pulled back. Three star-shaped chevrons highlighted the positions of the new alien attackers. Suddenly, three flashes of energy surged towards them and the Revocater was hit. The impacts sounded like the distant rumble of thunder, but Liberty somehow knew the attack had inflicted damage to the ship. However, she could not get a sense of how bad it was.

"Minor damage... initiating repairs," came the ethereal voice of Morphus, "I am attempting to return fire. Stand by..."

Liberty waited, but nothing happened. She was about to call out to Morphus, when one of the chevrons flashed and grew larger. She checked her consoles, but she could already instinctively sense the danger. One of the infiltrators had locked in a collision course.

"Turn away," said Morphus, its voice sounding weaker than ever. "You must evade the infiltrator. A direct collision at this velocity will penetrate the hull."

"Can't you shoot back?" Liberty called out, but there was no response. Fighting back the swell of panic in her gut, Liberty turned the Revocater away from the pursuing infiltrators, and the ship's mysterious propulsion system immediately altered their trajectory. It was like the Revocater was an enormous aircraft carrier navigating the open seas.

"Morphus, it's still gaining on us!" Liberty called out, as there were more flashes of energy, and more distant rumbles. "Morphus, shoot them!"

"I... am... unable..." said Morphus. "Try to... reach the... portal."

A collision warning sounded, and Liberty attempted to push the Revocater's mighty engines harder, but it seemed that the more she asked of the ship, the greater the physical toll was, both on Morphus and on her own body. Her arms were growing weak and she was now struggling to hold their course, as if the vacuum of space had suddenly turned into thick treacle.

"What's going on?"

Liberty spun around to see Tobin standing behind her. The top half of his body was bare, but the injuries sustained when the seed drones had slashed into his flesh were gone. In their place was a skin-like covering of glowing, golden alien metal. It was like a magical vest of chainmail made from mithril, and it had clearly saved his life. Liberty anxiously checked the position of the approaching infiltrator, then turned back to Tobin, realizing that his sudden arrival could not have come at a more important time.

CHAPTER 19

Liberty sprang out of her seat and pulled Tobin into a tight embrace. "You're alive!" she cried out, before drawing back to inspect his curious new augmentations, which went far beyond her own modest enhancements. "Are you okay?" she added, "You're glowing a little more than usual..."

"I feel fine," said Tobin. "In fact, I feel amazing." Then he looked at the view on the screen, and became concerned. "Liberty, what's happening? Where are we? Where is Morphus?"

Liberty glanced at the screen and saw that the infiltrator was still gaining. She dropped back down into the pilot's seat and grabbed the controls, re-establishing her link to the ship. "There's too much to explain right now, but we're on the Revocater, and we're under attack," said Liberty. "There's a new kind of alien ship, and one of them is on a collision course."

"What can I do?" asked Tobin appearing beside Liberty and grabbing onto the empty second seat.

"I'm still working on that..." replied Liberty, as she tried to push the engines harder, but she had nothing more to give. She could also feel the impacts from the energy bolts more violently now. The infiltrator was targeting the Revocater's engines, but in less than a minute, it would collide with them. The impact would be like a meteor strike, crippling the ship and ending any hope of stopping Goliath.

Then Liberty had an idea. It was crazy, but in a world where she was able to pilot a space ship that was almost two hundred city blocks long, crazy had become the new normal.

"Get into the second seat," she called back to Tobin. "I've had a brainwave."

Tobin immediately jumped into the seat and sat there staring at Liberty, expectantly awaiting more instructions. "Okay, now what?" he said, throwing his arms out.

"Remember how Morphus programmed your brain and made you a skilled marksman?" said Liberty, smiling. Then she concentrated her thoughts onto Morphus, trying desperately to reach the entity, as if through telepathy. "Morphus, hand over weapons control to Tobin," she said out loud. There was no answer, and now the infiltrator was less than thirty seconds away. "Morphus! Give Tobin weapons control in the second seat, now!"

Suddenly the second seat reconfigured around Tobin and a new set of controls grew out of the alien metal. Liberty watched on in astonishment as the new configuration took shape, resembling a Sperry ball turret from an old B17 Flying Fortress. Tobin grabbed the gun controls and the alien metal – which now comprised a significant portion of his torso – began to glow brightly. Liberty again glanced at the scanner, and saw that there were only a few seconds remaining until the infiltrator collided with them.

"Tobin, shoot the damn ship already!" Liberty cried out.

With the ease and skill of a veteran World War Two gunner, Tobin turned the turret-like weapon towards the infiltrator and pulled the trigger. An image of the space outside the ship stayed with him as he turned, suspended in mid-air like a floating projection screen. Bolts of energy then rippled out towards the diamond-shaped ship, peppering it like shotgun pellets tearing through paper. The infiltrator exploded, sending seed ship fragments in all directions.

"Great shot!" cried Liberty, before checking on the location of the other two infiltrators. They were also still in pursuit, but much further behind. She smiled again and tightened her grip on the controls. "I'm done running from these spiky little assholes," she said, before throttling back and turning the Revocater to face the oncoming enemy ships. "There you go," Liberty said, cheerfully, "Target practice..."

Tobin still looked completely shell-shocked. "I'd like to say I don't know what to do, but somehow, I do!" he said. Glancing up at the image in front of him, the view zoomed in on the next nearest infiltrator. Tobin spun the turret and fired, destroying it as effortlessly as he had the first.

The last infiltrator then began to slow, and veer away. Whatever intelligence the ship possessed was enough to know it was facing a losing battle, but with the tables turned, Liberty now pressed the pursuit.

"Oh no you don't..." said Liberty, setting an intercept course, before again turning to Tobin. However, this time their new gunner needed no prompting. He aimed the turret and annihilated the infiltrator with a swarm of precisely-aimed energy bolts.

Tobin let out an excited whoop, and released the turret controls. The alien metal grafted into his body dimmed to a duller luster, and the turret sank away into the ship, leaving Tobin back in the second seat, as if nothing had happened. However, Liberty then noted that the consoles in front of Tobin altered to mimic the design of his own personal shuttle, rather than the second seat of the Orion.

"That was amazing!" said Tobin, leaping up and rushing over to Liberty.

"I'm moderately impressed," replied Liberty, though she couldn't hide the grin on her face. "What's with that old-fashioned gun turret, though? Did that come from your head, or from Morphus?"

Tobin shrugged, "Hey, I like ancient Second World War fighter and bomber aircraft," he said, sounding a little embarrassed. "It's a hobby..."

"You and I are going to get along just fine," said Liberty, smiling and looking down at the Royal Air Force cap badge that she'd fashioned into a belt buckle. She then resumed course to the portal, but kept their velocity at a steadier pace, now the immediate threat was gone. However, the engines still felt strained, and it still required more effort than normal to hold the ship on course.

"Don't we already get along?" replied Tobin, still buzzing from the experience, but then he frowned and looked around the chamber. "Hey, speaking of Morphus, where is she?"

"Greetings, Tobin Rand entity," said Morphus.

Tobin literally jumped into the air, and spun around. The alien entity was now standing in front of him.

"Jeez, Morphus, you nearly gave me a heart attack," Tobin gasped, pressing a hand to his newly repaired chest.

"That is highly unlikely," replied Morphus, dryly. "The augmentations to your upper body include significant enhancements to your cardiovascular system. I calculate that these systems could sustain you for approximately three hundred and thirty-two of your Earth years."

"That's great," replied Tobin, looking genuinely excited about the prospect of an extended life, but then he scowled. "What about the rest of me, though?"

"Your other organic parts will decay as normal," said Morphus, maintaining its matter-of-fact delivery, and Tobin's face fell.

Liberty laughed and pushed herself out of her seat, before stepping up to Morphus and throwing her arms around it. "Welcome back, Morphus," she said, warmly. "I thought we'd lost you for a moment."

Morphus initially appeared to be confused by Liberty's gesture, but then tentatively returned the embrace.

"For a moment, I was lost," Morphus admitted. "The strain on my systems caused a temporary loss of function. You might call it a 'crash' in terms you understand." Liberty drew back, and the alien entity met Tobin's eyes. "However, your idea to enlist the Tobin Rand entity to manage another function of the Revocater's systems was inspired. It freed up enough of my own resources to manage the remaining functions of the vessel." Morphus attempted a smile, which looked a little plasticine, but was better than previous efforts. "You saved us, Tobin Rand entity. Thank you."

Tobin did a little bow, "You're welcome, though, it seems I was only returning the favor," he replied, looking down at his glowing skin. "Thanks for not leaving me back on the Corporeals' planet."

"My purpose is to protect corporeal life," said Morphus, stiffly, but then with a more human touch, it added, "However, you are welcome."

Liberty turned back to the screen wall and stared out at the peaceful sea of stars. "How bad is the damage to the Revocater?" she asked, directing the question to Morphus. "Can we still continue our transit to Earth?"

Morphus became absent for a second, as its consciousness filtered through the ship. Then it said, "We sustained minor damage to seven per cent of the vessel. Repairs are proceeding. We are still able to transit."

Liberty's console bleeped, and she checked it, discovering that the next portal was coming up ahead. "Speaking of transits, where do we end up next?" asked Liberty, dropping into the pilot's seat, and reducing speed to set them up for the transit.

"This portal will take us to System 5118208," answered Morphus.

Liberty and Tobin turned to the alien entity, both with haunted looks on their faces. "The next jump takes us to Earth?" asked Liberty. She had not been keeping count of their transitions, and somehow had still considered them to be a long way from home. Now the reality of what they were about to face hit her like a freight train.

"The portal will bring us out above the fourth planet in System 5118208," replied Morphus. "The body you call Mars."

Liberty puffed out her cheeks and blew out a heavy sigh, "Damn, I somehow thought we'd have more time." Then she glanced back at Morphus; her expression had adopted a harder edge. "Are we ready?"

Morphus stood between the two chairs and looked out into space. "We are ready," it said, confidently, before the entity met Liberty's eyes. "However, without the crystal, the Revocater is ill-equipped to face Goliath."

Liberty nodded, and turned back to her controls. "Let's all hope that Hudson has managed to get it back then," she said, while making the final adjustments for the transit.

Tobin sat in the second seat and together they waited for the imminent flash of light and swirling purple vortex.

"Transitioning in five, four, three, two, one... now," said Liberty.

The Revocater passed into the portal, blanketing the chamber in vivid purple tones. Then the darkness of space returned, but instead of an empty void ahead of them, Liberty saw the distinctive butterscotch color of Mars. They'd arrived far closer to the red planet than she'd expected, yet something immediately felt off. It was another sensation that seemed to stem from her connection to the Revocater, but she'd yet to fully master how to interpret them.

Then as if confirming her suspicions, Liberty's consoles began to flash and bleep angrily. "What the hell?" she said, unable to make sense of it all. She turned to Morphus for clarification, "What's going on?"

Morphus frowned, replicating the expression with practiced precision. "The Martian corporeals have assembled a war fleet," it said, as the view ahead zoomed in on a taskforce of dozens of MP cruisers, gunboats, destroyers and more.

"But that's good, right?" said Tobin, wondering why Morphus still appeared to look concerned.

The entity peered at Tobin, and then at Liberty. "I am afraid that the fleet has mistaken us for Goliath," said Morphus, "and they are mobilizing to attack."

CHAPTER 20

Morphus' alarming statement shook Liberty like an earthquake, and she hastily read the navigation scanner to check the movements of the MP fleet. She saw that the two hundred and ten MP vessels that were amassed around Mars were now breaking into combat groups, and heading their way.

"But why are they coming after us?" asked Tobin, also sounding alarmed. "Surely they can see that this ship isn't Goliath?"

Liberty noted that their portal entry point had placed Mars and the fleet between the Revocater and Earth. Liberty was familiar with the known Martian portal locations, including the one she and Hudson had discovered. However, from their position, it appeared that they had transited through a previously undiscovered portal. It was no wonder the Martian fleet had been spooked, she thought to herself.

"I guess one giant alien ship looks much the same as another," replied Liberty, turning the Revocater to face the approaching taskforce. "And it's not like we rang ahead to say we were dropping by..."

"Can't we just send the flagship a message?" suggested Tobin. "To tell them we're not a threat and are here to help?"

Morphus folded its arms, and shook its head, "I calculate a two percent chance that the corporeal fleet commander, Admiral Shelby, would believe such a statement," it said.

Tobin shrugged, "Two percent is better than nothing!"

Suddenly the view ahead zoomed in on one of the larger MP cruisers. Tactical information on the ship appeared alongside it, then a message from the vessel was relayed into the chamber.

"Unidentified alien vessel, this is Admiral Shelby of the Martian Protectorate," the message began. The severe, no-nonsense intonations of Shelby were unmistakable. "Withdraw immediately from this star system, or we will deem your presence to be hostile and attack."

Tobin shook his head, "Trust a Martian to assume an alien would understand English."

"I think we should be more concerned about the Martian weapons, rather than their arrogance," replied Liberty. Then she realized she didn't know how much of a threat the Martian fleet actually posed to the Revocater. Turning to Morphus, she said, "Should we be concerned? I mean, can that fleet actually do any serious damage to this ship?"

The view ahead zoomed out again, and all two hundred and ten ships were marked out as red chevrons. Morphus appeared to be lost in its own thoughts again, and Liberty realized it was conducting a thorough scan, in order to answer her question.

"Based on my analysis, this fleet's projectile-based weapons are capable of delivering minor damage to the Revocater's outer hull," said Morphus. "Yet it would require the entire fleet, sustaining continual, concentrated fire at a specific section of the ship to result in any serious impairment to the Revocater's functions."

Tobin seemed pleased by this response. "So, basically no then?" he said, smiling, but Morphus had not yet finished its analysis.

"However, I have also determined that ten of the Martian vessels also carry thermonuclear devices," Morphus continued, and Tobin's face fell. "But for these devices to have a significant destructive effect, they would need to penetrate the vessel's armor and detonate inside the Revocater. The likely outcome of their use is an electromagnetic pulse that would disable their own fleet, and irradiate their corporeal crews."

"So, you're saying even a nuke couldn't take us out?" asked Liberty.

Morphus shook its head. "We would sustain moderate damage, but no. Unfortunately, my previous assessment of the corporeal named Shelby suggests she would risk a nuclear assault, rather than allow us to proceed."

"Great," said Liberty, shaking her head. "So, the Martians can't attack us without destroying themselves in the process. What can we do?"

Morphus pointed to the view ahead, which switched to show a display of the solar system. Their location and that of the Martian fleet remained, but there was also a blue circle and several purple markers.

"The blue icon indicates Earth's current position relative to Mars," said Morphus. "The purple are local portals." Then the map zoomed out to show portal locations in other parts of the galaxy within a few hundred light years. A line extended from the solar system through some of these portals, and then back again. "I calculate that we can circumvent Mars by making three additional jumps, culminating in our arrival close to Earth's orbit."

Liberty looked at the map, and checked the position of the Martian fleet on her consoles. It was still moving towards them, with the largest cruisers in the vanguard.

"I don't see that we have a choice," said Liberty, locking in the first portal waypoint and grasping the controls. "I just hope that the detour doesn't allow Goliath to reach Earth before we do."

Morphus didn't respond. The entity appeared to have frozen again, as if it had departed its physical form and become one with the ship. Liberty and Tobin exchanged nervous glances, but Liberty continued on their new course.

Then the consoles in front of both of them registered an alert. Liberty instinctively looked back to Morphus for an explanation, but the alien was still statuesque. Instead she nervously read the new information on the console, hoping for the best, but expecting the worst.

"It's a Shaak radiation burst," said Liberty, frowning. "But it's massive. I haven't seen anything produce a spike like this other than a…" Liberty didn't finish her sentence. Her stomach turned over, understanding what the spike meant. She peered up at the screen, desperately hoping that she was wrong.

"Liberty, what is it?" said Tobin. His voice was unsteady and full of fear.

There was a huge flash of light, almost as if all of the nuclear warheads in the MP fleet had detonated simultaneously. It was followed by a swirling purple vortex; but one that was many times larger than Liberty had ever seen before. Then a ship began to emerge from the portal. At almost three times the size of the giant Revocater, it dwarfed the Martian fleet, making even the largest MP cruisers look like toy models in comparison.

Liberty felt her hands start to shake, and she gripped the control column even more tightly to steady them. Then she turned to Tobin and said, "It's Goliath. Goliath is here..."

CHAPTER 21

Goliath powered its gargantuan frame through the portal and the swirling purple vortex snapped shut behind it. Partially blinded by the intense glow of the great ship's transit, Liberty could at first see only a huge emptiness, like a black hole. Then, as her eyes adjusted and Goliath turned, catching the light from the sun, Liberty saw the malevolent vessel clearly. Somehow, the great ship looked even more menacing than the previous times she'd seen it. It was like a dark storm cloud hanging over the planet, threatening hostility.

"But where did it come from?" asked Tobin, peering down at the navigation scanner. "This chart doesn't show another portal over Mars, and Morphus must know where they all are."

Liberty glanced up at Morphus, who was still frozen, then checked the navigation scanner herself, "You're right, there isn't a portal in that location. I don't understand it..."

"So how the hell did it get here?" said Tobin, his voice pitchy and unsteady.

"Goliath has discovered how to generate its own long-range portals," said Morphus. Liberty spun around and was relieved to see that the entity had finally returned to life. "It is no longer limited to travelling through the established conduits created by the Corporeals."

"But why is it here, now?" asked Liberty. "Has it come for us, or for Mars?"

Morphus contemplated the question for a moment, but the quizzical expression on its simulated face suggested it did not know the answer. "The great ship's behavior has become unpredictable," it finally said, not answering the question. Then it looked at Liberty, and added, "The best tactical decision now would be to expedite our journey to Earth, and rendezvous with the Hudson Powell entity. Without the crystal, it would be futile to make a stand here."

Liberty shook her head, "But we can't leave the Martians to face Goliath alone," she said, already turning the Revocater back towards the red planet. "With our help, the MP fleet might have a chance!"

Morphus rested a hand on Liberty's shoulder, and peered into her eyes. It was as if the alien were consoling Liberty over the loss of a loved one.

"I calculate less than an eighteen percent chance we can overcome Goliath at this moment," the entity said. "If we fail here, everything is lost."

Liberty gritted her teeth and stared back at the screen. Either by choice or by accident, Goliath had emerged in the dead center of the Martian fleet. It had already ploughed through two of the heavy cruisers like they were bugs hitting the radiator grille of a truck, and its swarm of seed ships had shot out and cut through twenty other vessels. At its current rate of destruction, Liberty guessed the MP fleet would last only a matter of minutes.

"We have to try," said Liberty, holding her course towards the great ship. "I learned on the streets that if you run away from bullies, they keep coming back, but punch them in the face, and they think twice about attacking you again."

Tobin turned towards Liberty, while keeping half an eye on Goliath as it grew larger on the screen. "Liberty, this isn't the mean streets of San Francisco, and that ship isn't a common bully," he said, rushing through his words. "Morphus is right, we need to be smart. Mars may be lost, but we can still save Earth, and what's left of the other portal worlds. But we *have* to get that crystal."

Liberty would not be swayed. "We only have to force it to withdraw," she insisted. "It will at least buy us some time."

For several seconds no-one spoke, as both Liberty and Tobin waited for Morphus' decision. Ultimately, it was the alien AI's determination to make. It could override Liberty's control at any moment, if it wished to.

Eventually, Morphus turned to Liberty and said, "Very well, Liberty Devan entity. We will attempt to 'punch Goliath in the face', and force it to withdraw." Liberty clapped her hands together, and grabbed the controls again. "But..." Morphus added, ominously, "I cannot risk the Revocater being destroyed. If it becomes clear that Goliath will not withdraw, then we must."

Liberty nodded, "Agreed," she said, before glancing over at Tobin. "And how about you, nose gunner? Are you game for more target practice?"

Tobin shrugged and grabbed his controls. Once again, his station transformed into the curious alien adaptation of a gun position on a B17 Flying Fortress. "Even without my augmentations, it would be pretty hard to miss that thing," he said. Then he smiled, and added, "and this is technically more like a ball turret than a nose gun, by the way."

Morphus sank into its pod, and the thrum of the Revocater's massive reactors intensified. Liberty guessed they were going to need to hit Goliath with everything they had, just to get its attention.

"Okay, let's show this leviathan that we mean business," said Liberty. Then the navigation scanner chimed an alert and she saw that dozens of seed ships were incoming. "Some small fry, inbound," she called over to Tobin.

"On it," came the reply from the gunner. The view ahead and all around had already lit up the comparatively tiny targets. A second later, Tobin had unleashed a barrage of energy, shooting out in dozens of directions at dozens of targets. Each bolt struck true, destroying the seed ships with ease.

"I'm going to put us between the MP fleet and Goliath," said Liberty, steering the Revocater into the heart of the fight. "It might offer them some protection."

"And who is going to protect us?!" shouted Tobin, as his pod spun wildly in all directions.

"Less talking, more shooting!" replied Liberty, as she maneuvered the huge Revocater into position. Checking the scanner again, she saw that the MP vessels were falling in behind them. "It looks like they've realized we're not the enemy, after all," commented Liberty, smiling.

Tobin spun the gun pod towards the great ship, and focused all of the Revocater's hundreds of weapons on it. The thrum of the reactors rose to a crescendo, and Liberty could feel the enormous energy of the ship tingling through her body.

"Right, let's pop this bully on the nose and see what happens," Tobin said, tightening his grip. "Firing..."

Hundreds of bolts of energy shot out ahead, lighting up space like a New Year's Eve fireworks show. The bolts raked across Goliath's hull, and Liberty cheered, as she saw chunks of metal fracture away from the colossal ship, leaving a smoldering welt, as if it had been struck with a giant, red-hot poker.

"Shoot it again!" cried Liberty, feeling that they might actually have a chance, but Tobin looked suddenly tired, like he'd just woken up.

"Man, I feel like I haven't slept in a week," said Tobin, pushing himself upright. He then pressed the trigger again, but nothing happened. "I think the weapons are recharging," said Tobin, slumping back in his seat. "I hit that thing with everything we had, and it was just a slap in the face!"

Liberty looked out as Goliath then began to turn towards the Revocater, like a blue whale squaring off against a great white shark. Suddenly, the controls went dead in Liberty's hands, and the ship veered rapidly away.

"We have done what we can," came the voice of Morphus. "If we remain, Goliath will destroy us."

Liberty thrust herself back in her seat and cursed in frustration. "We almost had it!" she yelled.

"I think we only pissed it off," said Tobin. He had regained some of his strength, and was still able to pick off the seed ships, but his firing capacity was severely diminished.

Then the Revocater began to physically shake, like a car on the verge of stalling. Liberty gripped the arms of the chair, and peered out at the image of Goliath, slowly receding into the distance behind them. "What's going on?" she called out.

"Unknown," replied Morphus.

Liberty and Tobin looked at each other, eyes wide. If Morphus didn't know, then whatever was happening couldn't be good, Liberty thought. Then she noticed that the Shaak radiation levels were spiking again nearby. The levels weren't as high as when Goliath had arrived, but were still an order of magnitude higher than a portal transition for any human-made vessel. Liberty frowned at the number; she'd seen a similar Shaak radiation level somewhere before. Then she realized where; it almost precisely matched the value she'd observed when the Revocater had transited from system to system.

"Wait, I think Goliath is opening a portal!" cried Liberty. She was looking at Tobin when she spoke the words, but the statement was really intended for Morphus.

"Is it leaving?" said Tobin, hopefully.

"No," came the voice of Morphus. Never before had a single word struck so much terror into Liberty's heart. She knew what was happening; she could feel it through the ship itself. Goliath was casting a portal at the Revocater. It was doing to Morphus exactly what the alien AI had done to Goliath, millennia earlier – banishing it to a distant part of the galaxy.

There was a flash of light and the familiar purple vortex, but this time it felt like Liberty's entire head was spinning. Her eyes darkened, and she could feel herself losing consciousness. In her mind, she could hear Morphus and Tobin, but she could feel something else too, something primal and saturated with pure, unadulterated rage. And there was something more; a hateful satisfaction, and the thrill of vengeance.

Liberty opened her eyes, and discovered that she was slumped back in her seat. The view ahead showed that they were in normal space again, though the anonymous star-scape gave no hint as to where they were. She pushed herself up and saw that the consoles all seemed to be offline. The light level in the navigation hub chamber had also dropped, and the normally strident thrum of the enormous ship's reactors was muted, as if the ship had been drained of energy. Liberty felt fear grip her again, worried that the Revocater had been damaged as a result of being violently cast across space.

Liberty then glanced across to Tobin and saw that he was similarly woozy, but also starting to come around. She reached out and took hold of the controls, which came to life again in her hands, before immediately bringing the Revocater to a stop. *But where have I stopped?* she asked herself.

Morphus had banished Goliath to the center of the galaxy, but it had been required to sacrifice itself in the effort. And the fact was that Goliath was many times more powerful than Morphus; there may have been no limit to how far across the cosmos it had cast them.

"Morphus, are you there?" said Liberty, looking around the chamber for the alien entity. "Morphus!" she called again.

Tobin got up and called out too, but still there was no answer. "Do you think it's... dead?" said Tobin, but it was a question Liberty couldn't bear thinking about.

"What have I done?" cried Liberty, pressing her face into her hands. "I should have listened to Morphus. We should have left, and gone to Earth, like you said. Now everyone will die, and it's all my fault!"

"We are not defeated yet," said Morphus.

Liberty and Tobin span around to see the familiar female form of Morphus taking shape. Liberty almost collapsed.

"I thought you were dead," she said, pressing the backs of her hands to her eyes to squeeze away the wetness. "I thought that thing had stranded us on the other side of the galaxy, alone."

Morphus stepped between the consoles, and pointed to the far wall. The image switched to show a different star-scape, with a single, larger and brighter red mass in the center.

"That is Mars," said Morphus.

Liberty stood up and stared at the image in disbelief. "But that must be no more than a few hundred thousand kilometers away!" Liberty said, struggling to understand why Goliath had not cast them a far greater distance. She turned back to Morphus, and simply asked, "Why?"

Morphus again pointed to the screen, and the image of the red planet enhanced. "The great ship communicated with me," it explained to a rapt Liberty and Tobin. "It wants me to watch."

Liberty's console flashed, and she leant over to quickly read the new data. It showed two more radiation spikes. One read as gamma and neutron radiation, while the other was Shaak radiation. She looked back up at the screen and to her horror she could see that Mars was now breaking apart.

"No!" she cried out, but she knew it was true. She had felt Goliath's intentions too. It did not want to banish or destroy Morphus until its task was complete. And more than anything, it wanted Morphus to witness its failure.

"Mars has been destroyed, along with the entire Martian fleet," said Morphus, somberly. "Goliath is now heading to Earth."

Liberty ran to Morphus and grabbed the entity's shoulders. "But we can still make it to Earth first, can't we?" she cried, almost begging Morphus for the answer to be yes. "We can find a portal and jump there, before Goliath arrives!"

Morphus shook its head. "The closest portal is back at Mars. However, we do not require a portal in order to catch Goliath."

Liberty's head was spinning, and again all she could ask was, "Why?"

"Because Goliath wants us to catch it," said Morphus, coolly. "You have felt it yourself, Liberty Devan entity. It wants us to watch as Earth crumbles. Then it will take its final revenge upon me and this vessel. It will destroy the last Revocater, and then continue, unchallenged, to wipe out all sentient corporeal life in the galaxy."

Liberty shook her head, angrily. "Come on, there's still a chance," she insisted. "Hudson will get that crystal. He'll get the crystal and he'll meet us at Earth." She turned to face the image of Mars, now shattered and broken into billions of pieces. Her hands clenched into fists, and her alien augmentations glowed brightly. "Then we'll stop this monster, once and for all."

CHAPTER 22

After half a lifetime spent travelling the stars, the sight of a planet viewed from orbit was no more unusual to Hudson than a sunset, or a full moon. Yet of all the many planets he'd seen on his travels, there was always something special about Earth. He didn't know why; Earth was no more a home to him than a bunk in a spaceport, or a cabin on a freighter, but whatever the reason, he was glad of it. Hudson knew that Earth was far from perfect, and so was humanity, but for all its faults, it didn't deserve annihilation. Goliath had to be stopped, and they were fast running out of time.

The Orion's current destination was High Vegas, an orbital city that would serve as a quick and easy port, while they waited for Morphus to return. Hudson hated the place, but Ma and Tory had overruled, on account of it having the best bars in the solar system. And given the grim reality of their situation, Hudson couldn't argue with their logic; he could certainly use a good drink. He just hoped that High Vegas didn't end up being the venue where they witnessed the end of humanity, like a real-life version of the Restaurant at the End of The Universe.

"I've never seen so many ships in orbit before," said Tory, who had taken over piloting the Orion for the second leg of their journey back to Earth. "But after seeing what that alien ship can do, I can't see them even making a dent in it."

"We'd better just hope that Morphus manages to get that Revocater back here in time," replied Hudson, lounging back in the second seat. "And that we've cobbled together enough parts of a crystal for him to recombine a new one."

Suddenly, the console bleeped an incoming communications request.

"Speak of the devil?" asked Tory, with an inquisitive eyebrow raise.

Hudson shook his head, "No, it isn't Morphus," he replied, his rising tone betraying his surprise at who was actually calling. "It's Commodore Trent."

Tory huffed a laugh, "Perhaps he wants to press gang us into the war fleet."

Hudson shrugged, "Who knows, but if he's calling then I somehow doubt it's with good news," he said, sitting up and pulling on his headset. "I'll put it through on the speakers."

Hudson opened the channel, and Trent's voice immediately came through, loud and clear. "Orion, this is Commodore Trent. Is that you, Captain Powell?" Hudson glanced across to Tory, and from her apprehensive expression, he knew that she had detected the same abnormal tension in the Commodore's voice. Hudson had always thought Trent to be unflappable, but he was now sounding rattled.

"Yes, Commodore, this is Hudson Powell," replied Hudson, "I take it this isn't a social call?"

"No... I'm afraid not," came Trent's immediate and unsettling response. "What news of your alien ally?" he continued, getting straight to business.

"We haven't received word from them yet, but the long-range comms relays seem to be shot to hell at the moment," replied Hudson, "and we've only just arrived back in the solar system. I take it you've heard about Brahms Three?"

"Yes..." said Trent, again with the same, firm but disquieting brevity, "however the situation has recently become much worse. Mars has also been completely destroyed, along with the entire Martian taskforce." Hudson shot a nervous glance at Tory, and then forced down a dry swallow. "The alien vessel is now en route to Earth." Trent added, gloomily. "I fear that your ally is our only hope."

Hudson cleared his throat. "We'll try to contact them, Commodore, but they could be anywhere in the galaxy still," he said, wishing he had better news to offer. "Until they arrive back in this system, all we can do is wait."

"They may already have returned," said Trent, though the tone of his voice did not convey any hope. "We have very limited intel from Mars, but long-range scans picked up two distinct vessels, both many times larger than anything in either the CET or MP fleets," Trent continued. "There were reports that the smaller of the two engaged the one you call Goliath, but then it disappeared."

Hudson's mouth was now completely dry, and his heart was racing. "Did you say 'disappeared', Commodore? Disappeared where?"

There was an agonizing silence, before Trent answered. "We do not know." Then, more despairingly, he added, "We must consider the possibility that it was destroyed."

Hudson shook his head, "No, I'm not willing to accept that," he said, forcefully. "They wouldn't have engaged Goliath without the crystal. It's the only weapon that can defeat it."

There was another momentary silence, before Trent answered, "I hope you're right, Captain Powell, I really do." Then his demeanor became a touch more optimistic. "On the assumption your ally is still on the board, I also have news of the crystal you spoke of."

Hudson and Tory both sat up a little straighter at the mention of the crystal. Especially because it would also provide some insight into what happened to Cutler and Griff.

"We captured the RGF fugitive, Logan Griff, with his former commanding officer, Jane Wash," Trent continued.

Wash... it figures those two slime balls would end up together, Hudson thought to himself.

"The mercenary, Cutler Wendell, gave me the crystal and turned them over in exchange for a full pardon, but I am sorry to say he deceived me," Trent went on. "The crystal was a fake."

Tory slammed her fist on the console. "That lying, double-crossing piece of shit!" she called out.

"Quite..." replied Trent, though Hudson didn't think Tory had intended the Commodore to hear her outburst. "Logan Griff and Jane Wash also recently escaped custody, killing three guards in the process."

Tory threw her hands up in despair, but refrained from cursing this time. Hudson merely sighed and massaged the bridge of his nose. "Forgive my bluntness, Commodore, but I'm not hearing any good news here."

"Then allow me to give you some," Trent replied. "We have located Cutler Wendell's hideout. It seems he has a cabin up near Barnett Lake in Manitoba, Canada."

Hudson clenched a fist and shook it, triumphantly, "Finally, that is good news, thank you Commodore," said Hudson.

"Don't thank me yet, Captain," replied Trent, hurriedly. "Intelligence also reports that he may have done a second deal with what remains of the Council. I suspect this is who he intends to exchange the real crystal with. I hear that Mr. Wendell and the Council have some history."

Tory barked a derisive laugh, and muttered "That's an understatement and a half..."

"Understood, Commodore, but if that's the case, there may be no hope of getting it back," replied Hudson, while Tory's anger continued to stew.

"That may be so, but unfortunately, my forces must now move to intercept the alien vessel, Goliath," Trent continued. "Our other resources are already engaged in urgent rescue and humanitarian efforts for the survivors from the portal worlds. Given the likelihood that Cutler Wendell has already moved the crystal, if you go after him, I'm afraid you're on your own."

Hudson nodded, "I understand, Commodore."

"I'll transmit the coordinates to you now. Good luck, Captain Powell," said Trent.

"To both of us, Commodore," replied Hudson. "Orion, out."

Hudson closed the channel and pulled the headset off, before flopping back in his seat. He glanced over at Tory, and saw the wrought iron determination forged into her expression. He'd seen the same look a dozen times before, and he already knew what she wanted to do.

"He's probably already sold the crystal to the Council, you know," said Hudson, skipping straight to the crux of the matter. "And there's a chance what we have is already enough."

"We're going after him," said Tory, resolutely. "Honestly, I don't care if he's sold it, made it into a necklace or even if he's shoved it up his ass. We're going after that bastard."

Hudson laughed, "If he's shoved it up his ass, then I'm definitely not retrieving it."

The door to the cockpit slid open and Ma walked in, yawning. She'd been using Liberty's cabin to get some rest and recover from her injuries. Noticing the grim expressions on the faces of Hudson and Tory, she scowled. "Okay, so what did I miss?".

"We're going to Canada to pull an alien crystal out of the ass of Cutler Wendell," said Hudson, smirking slightly.

"I'm not even going to ask," replied Ma, waving a hand at them, dismissively. "Just find me a weapon, and wake me when we've landed," she added, before closing the door, and heading back to her bunk.

CHAPTER 23

Hudson set the Orion down in a clearing behind a ridge, a kilometer away from the coordinates Commodore Trent had given them. He'd approached low and slow, so as not to attract any attention, but their longer-range scans of the area had suggested three ships were already landed nearby. Hudson guessed that one of them was likely to be Cutler's shuttle, with the other two being Council vessels.

"Ma, are you sure you don't want to sit this one out?" asked Hudson, as the rear ramp of the Orion finished lowering. "You're already pretty beat up and shot to hell as it is."

"I'm fine," said Ma, slapping Hudson on the shoulder and knocking him off balance, thanks to her brute strength. "With the drugs I found in your medical bay, plus a few slugs of my whiskey, I can't feel a damned thing right now." Then she pointed to the pistol showing just inside Hudson's jacket. "I'm going to need one of those, though."

Tory jumped down onto the deck and removed her Colt Frontier Six Shooter. Spinning it around in her hand, she then offered it to Ma. "You can use this, if you'd like?"

Ma took the weapon and inspected it, with a perplexed frown. "Damn, this thing is even older than I am," she said. "It's a beaut', but I'm afraid I'm not really au fait with the classics."

Then Hudson remembered that he still had Griff's old sidearm in a locker. It was the one Griff had dropped after their fight on the alien space station. He walked over to where he remembered stashing it, and after a few seconds of rummaging around, he found it.

"Maybe this is more your style?" said Hudson, holding out the weapon.

Ma gave the six-shooter back to Tory and took the sidearm from Hudson. "This is an RGF-issue piece," she said, surprised. "Did they not take yours back after you were kicked out?"

"For the last time, Ma, I quit before they fired me!" replied Hudson, snippily, before adding, "But yes, they did take it back. This is Logan Griff's old weapon. He dropped it during one of our earlier encounters."

Ma nodded, appreciatively, and then shoved the weapon into her waistband. "I look forward to reintroducing him to it someday," she said, with a wry smile.

They all stepped outside, and for a few seconds, they were struck by the sheer beauty of the place. Even Tory seemed to be impressed by the clear, sparkling water and rocky, wooded terrain that stretched for miles in all directions.

"I'm glad this Goliath didn't decide to invade in winter," commented Ma, zipping up her jacket to the collar. "Otherwise, we'd be trekking through snow."

Hudson led the way, using a small datapad to guide them. The stunning Manitoba scenery and serene peacefulness of the place almost made Hudson forget about everything that was happening. However, after trekking for fifteen minutes, they reached the top of a shallow, tree-lined hill, and got their first sight of the hideout. The jet-black Council transports parked nearby instantly brought Hudson crashing down to reality.

"If it wasn't for the Council ships blotting the landscape, this would be one hell of a place for a holiday," said Hudson, looking at the idyllic log cabin, which sat on the edge of a perfectly clear lake.

"You have to be kidding? It's too damn cold," complained Ma, "and what's that smell in the air?"

Hudson frowned at her, "You mean 'freshness'?" he said, remembering that Ma was used to the sticky heat and pungent smell of Brahms Three's scavenger town.

"That one doesn't look like a council ship," said Tory, nodding towards a third, much smaller vessel near the cabin.

There was a flyer pad a little off to the side, and Hudson could see a dilapidated-looking shuttle parked there. There were also three men in suits standing outside, and Hudson recognized the cut of their clothes immediately.

"No, but I'd know those suited goons anywhere," Hudson replied.

The door to the large cabin opened, and three more suited Council goons walked out. They took over from the men who were outside, shaking hands and bumping fists with each other lazily, before the original three entered the cabin instead.

"Looks like a changing of the guard," said Hudson. "Which means we're looking at a minimum of six guards, plus Cutler Wendell, and who knows how many others inside." He let out a sigh and turned to Tory and Ma. "I don't really like our odds."

"I've faced worse," said Tory, with a slight shrug. Coming from anyone else, Hudson would have considered it an exaggerated boast, but with Tory the chances were it was true. "On the plus side, if the Council is still here, then likely Cutler hasn't made the exchange yet," Tory added. "They could be doing it right now."

Suddenly, there was a sharp crack of dry twigs snapping. It came from the trees below them. Tory drew her six-shooter and Ma drew her pistol.

"I'll circle around behind," whispered Tory. "See if you can draw them out, but then take cover behind these rocks. And stay out of sight of that cabin."

Hudson and Ma nodded, and Tory slipped away into the woodland. Hudson and Ma slid down and crouched behind some rocks. Hudson could clearly see shadows moving through the trees towards them. Then two figures rushed out, weapons raised, and took aim at the rocks that Hudson and Ma were hiding behind. To Hudson's astonishment, the two figures were Logan Griff and Jane Wash.

"Out you come, nice and slow," growled Griff, but then he recognized Hudson and lowered his weapon a fraction. "Hudson Powell?" he said, as incredulously as if he'd just seen Santa Claus in front of him. "What the hell are you doing here, rook?"

Wash then stepped forward, looking just as perplexed as Griff. "You've got some explaining to do," she said, training her pistol on Hudson.

There was the distinctive sound of a Winchester being cocked, then Tory appeared behind Wash and Griff. "You first," said Tory, aiming the rifle at Griff's back.

Hudson and Ma quickly raised their weapons, Hudson aiming at Wash, and Ma at Griff. Recognizing that she was outnumbered and had been outflanked, Wash immediately dropped her weapon and thrust up her hands in surrender.

Griff shook his head, "What the hell happened to 'no half measures'?" he grumbled, reluctantly also raising his hands, but keeping hold of his pistol. "With a spine like that, it's a wonder you can stand upright."

"Shut up, clobber," snapped Ma, moving in and taking Griff's weapon, while Tory stepped around to face them.

"Powell doesn't interest me," Wash said glancing back at Griff, before turning to Hudson. "We're only here for Cutler Wendell. I assume that's also why you are here?"

"We want the crystal that Cutler, and that lowlife asshole..." Hudson wafted his pistol at Griff, "...stole from my ship." Then he took a step towards Griff and squared off against him. "And I haven't forgotten what you did to Liberty either, you piece of shit."

Griff glowered back at him, his eyes reflecting Hudson's contempt like a mirror. "She got what she deserved, rook," he snarled, "and I'm far from finished with you, too."

Hudson snapped and threw a fast right cross, which connected solidly with Griff's jaw and sent him to the ground. Then he stood over his former partner and aimed his pistol at his head.

Griff spat blood onto the rocks and then smiled up at Hudson. "Don't make me laugh, rook," he said, taunting Hudson. "We both know you don't have it in you. It's why you'll never beat me."

Surprisingly, it was Wash that intervened. "I don't blame you for wanting to kill him," said Wash, cautiously stepping in front of Hudson. "Hell, I'd happily pull the trigger for you. But how about we hold off killing each other, until we get the man we all came here for?"

Griff pulled himself up and sat on a rock, dabbing blood from his split lip onto his sleeve. "What's with all this 'we' crap?" he said, still glowering at Hudson.

"I propose a deal," said Wash, sounding like the politician she was. "The enemy of my enemy is my friend. We help each other to overpower the Council, who we both know are over in the cabin."

Tory laughed, and rested the Winchester over her shoulder. "Why the hell would we trust either of you two? And what do you get out of it?"

Wash seemed immediately more confident; dishing out plans and orders was her home turf. "It's really very simple," she began, in her prickly and patronizing tone of voice. "We help you to retrieve the crystal, and in return you lobby Commodore Trent on our behalf."

Hudson frowned, "Commodore Trent? What does he have to do with this?"

"I know you are in contact with Trent, and even have some influence with him," Wash continued. "Give me your word that you will petition Trent to exonerate us, and we'll help you get the crystal."

Griff was now listening with interest. The fact he hadn't rudely interrupted or insulted Wash's idea meant he gave it merit. However, while Hudson didn't care about Wash, he wasn't about to let Griff off the hook for everything he'd done.

"He doesn't get to have a clean slate," replied Hudson, pointing at Griff. "Not after everything he's done."

Wash pressed her hands behind her back and fixed Hudson with her steel-blue eyes. "What do you value more, Mr. Powell?" she said, clearly building up to her planned punchline. "Does your desire for revenge supersede your need to recover the crystal?"

Tory then moved quickly and pressed the barrel of the Winchester to Griff's head. "The four of us are enough," she said, slipping her finger onto the trigger. "We don't need this piece of shit."

Hudson sighed and closed his eyes. As much as he wanted Griff to pay for what he'd done, Wash was right. They needed all the help they could get. And killing Griff in cold blood would make them no better than he was.

"Tory, wait," said Hudson, though it was more of a struggle than he'd expected to say those words. "As much as I hate to admit it, Wash is right. We need their help."

Griff grinned, "That's right, obey your new master," he sneered at Tory, but the smirk was smartly wiped off his face, as Tory drilled the steel toe of her boot into Griff's groin. The RGF officer buckled and crumpled to the floor, paralyzed in agony to the level where he couldn't even manage to utter a whimper of pain.

"His time will come, Tory," said Hudson, as Tory adjusted her furious gaze towards him. "Even if Trent pardons him, it just means he escapes some jail time. It doesn't mean that it's all square between us."

Wash smiled at the writhing form of Logan Griff, apparently deriving some perverse pleasure from his pain, then held out a hand to Hudson. "So, Mr. Powell, do we have a deal?"

Hudson shook his head, but took Wash's hand. The sensation of her clammy, cold skin made him feel immediately dirty. "We have a deal," he said. Wash then tried to pull her hand away, but Hudson held onto it, and pulled the woman towards him. "But if you even think about double-crossing us, I'll kill you myself," he added. The menacing growl of his voice was similar to his 'tough guy relic hunter' persona. Except this time, Hudson wasn't play acting.

CHAPTER 24

To Hudson's amazement, agreement over a plan to attack the cabin had been reached without any major squabbling or disagreement. Despite Tory's suggestion that simply shooting up the place would be the simplest option, no-one else wanted to get involved in a gun battle, especially as the Council goons had significantly more firepower. And with five of them, and only three guards outside at any one time, the unlikely allies had the advantage of numbers and surprise.

The plan was to conduct a sneak approach through the trees, then subdue the guards before they realized what had hit them. With the guards down, they would then storm the hut, and hope whoever was inside also preferred not to have a close-quarters shootout. It wasn't the most bullet-proof plan that Hudson had ever heard in his life, but they were out of options, and rapidly running out of time. Goliath was already on its way to Earth, and after making short work of Admiral Shelby's powerful war fleet, he doubted Trent's forces would fare much better.

At Hudson's insistence, Griff and Wash moved out ahead. Despite Wash's bargain, he still didn't trust her as far as he could throw her, and he reckoned he could probably throw the petite woman quite far. However, he was relying on the corrupt politician's instinct for self-preservation to overshadow any treacherous thoughts she may have. Griff, on the other hand, Hudson wasn't taking his eye off even for a second.

They reached a position at the edge of the tree line and waited for the one guard who was actually patrolling the veranda to saunter off. With no other soul for fifty miles in any direction, the Council goons had obviously grown bored, and were taking their duties less than seriously.

"Okay, move out, just like we planned," said Hudson, holding his pistol ready. "Get their weapons, gag and bind them, then get ready to move inside, nice and smooth."

"I heard the plan the first time, rook," snarled Griff. He clearly took offence at taking orders from his former rookie. "Just make sure you don't screw up this job, like you screwed up at the RGF."

Hudson felt an urge to punch Griff in the face again, but buried the feeling, along with his other murderous impulses.

"Just do your part, asshole, and we'll do ours," Hudson retorted. "Now move."

Griff and Wash waited for the guard to move off and slump down lazily onto a deck chair. They both then crept forward, with Hudson and the others behind, moving around to tackle the other two lackadaisical guards. Suddenly Tory stopped, and held out her arm.

"What is it?" whispered Hudson, watching as Tory tentatively inspected the ground ahead of them.

"Stop, there are traps!" Tory hissed, trying to get the attention of Wash and Griff, but it was already too late.

Griff turned around, just as Wash planted a size four boot on a pressure plate. There were several dull, pneumatic-sounding thuds, as projectiles were sprung out of their concealed launchers. A split-second later, there was a deafening bang, and Hudson was hit with a blinding flash of light.

The next thing Hudson knew he was on his back, with hands grabbing at his arms. His ears were ringing, and his eyesight was still hazy. He heard the distant sound of gunfire and tried to turn his head towards it, spotting a blurry shape running back into the woods. Then he heard voices, still fuzzy and indistinct, and felt himself being hauled to his knees.

Hudson's mind was still groggy, and his ears whined with a shrill tone, but his eyes had cleared and he could now see Tory and Ma beside him. A little further ahead of them was Jane Wash, also on her knees in the dirt. Griff was conspicuous by his absence. Hudson craned his neck, trying to see if his old partner was still face down in the dirt near Wash, but there was no sign of him. Then he remembered the shape running into the woods, and shook his head. *That has to be at least seven or eight of that bastard's nine lives gone...* he mused, realizing Griff had got away.

The rest of them were now surrounded by the suited Council goons, all armed with compact sub-machine guns. Then from out of the log hideout he saw two more men approaching. He hung his head, knowing at once that their situation had become even more dire. The first man he'd recognized as the notorious Council boss, Werner Nest. On his own, this was bad news, but the man walking alongside him was none other than Cutler Wendell.

CHAPTER 25

Werner stepped forward and examined each of the faces kneeling before him, before finally stopping at Hudson. Cutler hung back a couple of paces behind Werner; the mercenary's mouth was curled ever so slightly into a smile. For a man that was renowned for conveying very few emotions, he was doing an excellent job of looking smug, Hudson thought.

"Well, this *is* a pleasant surprise," said Werner, still looking at Hudson. He was speaking with a version of his 'kindly uncle' voice, but it was laced with a sinister conceitedness. "I had thought it would take longer to find you again, but here you are, delivered to me on a plate. And with friends too. What a delightful gift."

Wash shrugged off the guard behind her and stood up, before taking a step towards Werner. The armed guards reacted instantly, thrusting their semi-automatic weapons at the former RGF commander. Wash stopped dead, eyeing the weapons uneasily, before speaking to Werner directly. "I am not with these people," she protested, before glaring at Cutler. "I only came for the mercenary, to get back what he stole from me."

Werner nodded, "Yes, Mr. Wendell is rather good at that. It is why we hire him." Then Werner pulled the alien crystal shard out of his pocket and held it up. "I believe this is the stolen item you are referring to?" Werner added, brightly. "Though as I understand it, you were not its original owner, either." Werner then peered down at Hudson, his entire face suddenly tensing up and becoming sharper. "I told you that I would get what I wanted, Mr. Powell. You should have listened, while you had the chance."

Hudson cut in, though he remained on his knees, careful not to aggravate any trigger-happy guards. "Werner, I need that crystal," he said, conveying the appropriate urgency. "The alien ship is heading to Earth right now. The entire planet will be destroyed if you don't give it to me; then it will be worth nothing to anyone."

Werner suddenly exploded, "I already told you that I do not care!" he roared, before taking several deep breaths. The Council boss waited until his red-faced anger had subsided, before continuing. "Apologies for the uncouth outburst, but I do find you intensely irritating, Mr. Powell," said Werner, more calmly.

Hudson almost laughed at how Werner had both apologized and insulted him in the same sentence. However, the Council boss's demented outburst motivated him to stay silent.

"If the CET military wants this item, then it will cost them dearly," Werner added. "I should say an entire planet or two, in fact."

This time Hudson was unable to stifle a laugh, before shaking his head. "You're insane, Werner. The Outer Portal Worlds are gone, along with half a dozen CET planets, and – in case you hadn't noticed – Mars too. There won't be any habitable planets left if Goliath isn't stopped, and you'll be dead, just like the rest of us."

Werner's jaw tightened, and he looked to be on the verge of another outburst, but this time he managed to keep a lid on his anger. "Some of us will die sooner than others, Mr. Powell," he threatened, his right eye twitching as the words escaped his lips. Then Werner slowly removed a sidearm from the holster of a suited goon to his side. "After all the trouble you have caused me, I was looking forward to killing you personally," he continued, raising the weapon and aiming it at Hudson's chest. "Unfortunately, in part-payment for delivering this crystal to me, I have ceded that honor to Mr. Wendell."

Wash suddenly stepped in front of Werner, blocking his view of Hudson. "Look, take me with you," she said, sounding slightly frantic. "I have powerful friends, and a whole datapad of dirty secrets to exploit. I could be of great use to your organization. I don't care what you do to the others. Kill them for all I care!"

Werner shifted the aim of the pistol and pulled the trigger, shooting Wash through the heart at point blank range. She fell inches away from Hudson, making him flinch as her body thudded to the ground and writhed weakly in the dirt. Hudson was unable to look away, rapt by the horrific scene in front of him, until Wash finally fell still.

"This abhorrent woman, however, was not part of my agreement with Mr. Wendell," said Werner. There was a dark serenity to his voice, as if the act of murder had helped to soothe his nerves. "Nor is the other woman that I see has joined your troupe," he added, looking across at Ma. "Though violence does bore me, so Mr. Wendell may kill her too if he wishes."

Ma looked ready to spring up and charge at Werner, but curiously it was Tory that held her back. Of all the people Hudson knew, Tory was the one he expected to be losing her cool and attempting a high-risk escape, but she appeared strangely focused and calm. Then Tory briefly met Hudson's eyes, before glancing sharply towards the ground in front of her. Hudson tracked her gaze and saw another metal pressure plate.

Another glimmer trap... Hudson realized, suddenly understanding why Tory had been so subdued. He quickly turned his eyes back to Werner, wary of drawing attention to the device.

Werner appeared not to have suspected anything, and casually handed the sidearm back to the guard. He then pressed his hands behind his back, and glanced at Cutler. "Well, Mr. Wendell, shall we conclude our business?"

Cutler smiled and stepped forward. Hudson saw that he had Tory's Colt Frontier six-shooter in his hand.

"It is a shame I won't get to kill Logan Griff at the same time, but that buffoon won't get far," Cutler began, patting the barrel of the weapon against his palm. Then he turned to Tory and shook his head, slowly. "No, using this would be too quick and easy," he said, tossing the weapon to the dirt like a piece of garbage, and drawing a knife from a scabbard on his belt. "Because of your betrayals, your death deserves to be slow and painful," he continued, his monotone voice full of bile. Then his eyes flicked across to Hudson. "And he is going to watch every second of your suffering."

Tory stood up, causing the guard behind her to flinch anxiously, then she slowly extended her arms out wide, as if surrendering to her fate. Her boot was now only a couple of inches from the concealed pressure plate.

"You've already stabbed me in the back once, like the coward you are," Tory said, locking eyes with Cutler. "But you didn't kill me then, and you're not going to kill me now."

Cutler aimed the tip of the blade a Tory. "I used to admire your unyielding tenacity," he snarled, "but now I just find you tiresome. Goodbye, Tory. And this time, it really is the end."

Tory smiled. "Yes, it is," she said, and stomped on the pressure plate.

Tory threw herself to the ground, squeezing her eyes shut and covering her ears. Hudson did the same, managing to close his eyes a fraction of a second before the glimmer detonated. Even with his quick reactions, Hudson wasn't fully shielded from the intense sound and flash of the stun weapon, and it was several seconds before he could get his bearings. He rose and saw Werner, lying on the ground. The Council boss had fallen against a cluster of rocks, and blood was pouring from a fracture to his skull. Cutler and the other guards had also fallen, but the Council goons that had been further from the blast were only lightly stunned, and already several were climbing back to their feet.

Tory wasted no time, stripping the sub-machine gun from the prone body of the guard to her rear, before ferociously kicking him in the head.

Ma also seemed to have suffered less from the effects of the glimmer. She was grappling with one of the other guards, and winning the fight.

Three of the other Council goons who had been further away from the glimmer trap opened fire, but while they were not as badly afflicted as those who were close to the explosion, they were still dazed and their aim was wild.

Hudson stayed low as the bullets whistled overhead, but Tory stood tall, defying the Council guards to shoot her. Incredibly, due to either fate or fortune, the storm of bullets all missed her. Separate volleys hit a guard near Hudson, while another sprayed across the back of the guard that Ma was fighting. The pair fell, and Ma was thrown against the rocks.

Hudson tried to run to Ma's side, but then Tory raised the sub-machine gun and opened fire at the guards, forcing him down again. Tory's aim was laser precise, and the remaining guards were all hit and killed instantly, before they had a chance to fully recover their senses.

As the sub-machine gun clicked empty, Cutler suddenly sprang up and pounced at Tory, tackling her to the ground. She fell hard, and the weapon slipped from her hands. In a near frenzy, and with his face contorted in rage, Cutler grabbed a rock and raised it above Tory's head. Hudson rushed at the mercenary and tackled Cutler a mere fraction of a second before he could crack Tory's head open like an egg.

Hudson and Cutler fought wildly, tumbling across the rocky terrain, grappling and punching at each other like savages. Then Cutler got the upper hand, managing to throw Hudson aside, before scrambling across the dirt to recover his knife.

"I should have killed you the first second I saw you!" snarled Cutler, aiming the blade at Hudson, and spitting blood onto the soil.

Hudson shook his head to clear it, then looked up to see the knife glinting in the sun. He was still on the ground, but there was something solid pressing against his leg. He shifted position slightly and saw that it was Tory's six-shooter.

"You have interfered in my affairs for the last time," Cutler growled, slowly stalking towards Hudson. "I would have preferred that you watched Tory die first, but I will settle for her reaction to me slitting your throat instead."

Hudson grabbed the six-shooter and aimed it at Cutler. "I'm afraid I'm going to have to disappoint you again," he said, pulling the hammer back.

Cutler stopped dead, glancing at the weapon, then back at Hudson, before he laughed. "You won't shoot me," he sneered. "It is like Griff always said. You don't have the guts."

Cutler advanced again, driving the blade towards Hudson, but then a single crack pierced the air. Hudson watched as Cutler Wendell pressed a hand to his chest, before seeing it soaked with blood. The mercenary held his hand up and peered at it, a look of complete bewilderment overtaking his normally expressionless face, before raising his eyes to Hudson. The look on his face then shifted, but it wasn't pain, or anger, or even surprise. It was a look of humiliation and embarrassment. Hudson lowered the smoking six-shooter to his side, as Cutler opened his mouth to speak, but no words came out. The mercenary fell forward, his face driving into the dirt. He twitched twice, and didn't move again.

Hudson continued to stare down at Cutler's body for a few seconds, before he noticed that Tory had shuffled across to his side.

"He won't be the last monster we kill before this is all over," said Tory, flatly. Then she held Hudson's shoulders and turned him towards her. "Hey, are you okay?"

Hudson flipped the six-shooter and slotted it back into Tory's holster. "I wish it hadn't come to this," he said, managing a weak smile. "But I won't be shedding a tear for Cutler Wendell."

Tory nodded, then walked up to where Werner Nest lay with his head cracked open against the rocks. "And no-one will miss this low-life either," she said, looking at the dead criminal impassively. She then crouched down and fished the alien crystal fragment out of the Council boss's pocket.

"I hope this thing is worth all the trouble it's caused," said Tory, returning to Hudson and holding out the crystal.

Hudson took the alien relic, and slipped it into his inside jacket pocket. "I think it's about time we find out," he replied. "I just hope that Trent was wrong about Morphus, and that they're on their way here too."

There was a groan from behind them, and both turned to see Ma getting up, rubbing her head. "What the hell hit me?" she said, groggily. "I feel like I drank an entire bottle of my own whiskey."

Hudson and Tory helped Ma to stand. Along with her wounded shoulder, she now had a dozen other knocks and a nasty cut to her head. It was likely she also had a concussion, Hudson guessed.

"If you'd drunk an entire bottle of your own whiskey, you'd be as dead as this lot," Hudson said, holding the veteran hunter's shoulders to help steady her.

Ma seemed not to hear Hudson's reply, and was instead blinking at the corpses lying all around them. She let out a low whistle. "Speaking of the dead, it looks like I missed the party."

Hudson nodded. "Most of it, but as parties go, this one wasn't much fun."

"What about that snake, Logan Griff?" asked Ma, wavering a little, so that Tory also had to hold her steady. "I see the other two scumbags, but not him."

Hudson looked off towards the tree line that he vaguely remembered Griff running towards, before the fight had started. "He's still out there somewhere," he said, wistfully. "But Griff will have to wait. We need to get this crystal to Morphus, before it's too late."

Ma let out a heavy sigh and rubbed her head again. "Let's get to it then," she said, trying to take a step forwards, but her legs immediately gave way.

"Woah, you've done more than enough, already, Ma," replied Hudson, throwing Ma's arm over his shoulder, and hauling her back upright. "I think you can sit this last part out."

Ma shrugged off the support of Tory and Hudson. "Don't talk nonsense, I'm fighting fit!" she protested. Ma again tried to head off towards the cabin, but staggered and nearly fell again, before Tory rushed forward to catch her.

"Just get me a weapon, and... show..." Suddenly Ma's words started to slur, and she became limp in Tory's arms.

Hudson helped Tory lowered Ma to the ground, before they rested her gently onto the grass.

"What's wrong?" said Hudson, meeting Tory's concerned-looking eyes. "Please tell me she's not dying?"

Tory slid her hand out from behind Ma's back. In it was a small device with a round head that ended in a sharp point. "It's like a sedative," explained Tory, waving the device at Hudson. "It's more designed for silent takedowns, but in this case, it's for obstinate, badly injured ex-relic hunters."

Hudson laughed, "You do realize that she's going to be mightily pissed off when she wakes up?"

Tory shrugged, "I know. But I also know what it's like to be as stubborn as a mule," she replied. "And you're right, she's in no condition to fight on."

Hudson looked around the site, before glancing up into the sky. There was still no sign of Goliath, but the air felt charged, as if a storm was on its way.

"We can set her down in the cabin, then head back to the Orion," said Hudson. "I sure as hell don't want to be around when she wakes up and realizes that we've gone without her."

Tory smiled, then also looked up into the sky. "Considering where we're going, what we need to do, and what we're about to face, I'd rather be in Ma's boots right now."

Hudson smiled and put his arm around Tory's waist. "Who are you trying to kid?" he said, coyly. "You wouldn't miss a chance to take down Goliath for all the bourbon in Kentucky."

CHAPTER 26

Hudson knew something was wrong from the moment he and Tory set foot back inside the cockpit of the Orion. They could see dozens of ships climbing into the air on the horizon all around their remote location, ignoring the laws and regulations that governed powered flight. The data from the navigation scanner painted an even grimmer picture. Thousands of ships were fleeing the cities all across Canada and the United States. It was like Brahms Three all over again, except the number of ships, and the degree of chaos, was amplified by an order of magnitude or more.

Hudson was in the second seat, since Tory had recovered more swiftly from the effects of the glimmers. She explained it as being due to the number of times she'd been hit with the stun weapons in her adventurous past. Continual exposure gave her a sort of acquired resilience to their effects, like how the body naturally builds up a resistance to common diseases.

While Tory lifted them into orbit, Hudson turned his attention from the navigation scanner to the news feeds. It was a mess of frantic reporting, with the only reliable data streams coming from the planet's surface. The armada of five hundred CET military vessels in orbit were clogging up the space-based comms stations and satellites, but the interference was still far more severe than he expected.

"I can't get a clear signal out to anyone through this EM soup," complained Hudson. "I've been trying to raise Commodore Trent, but all of the civilian channels are a mess."

"Oh shit..." said Tory.

This was not the reply Hudson was expecting, and he looked up from his console to see what had prompted Tory's perturbing reaction. He had been so engrossed in the news reports, and with trying to raise Commodore Trent, that he'd not looked outside for some time. What he saw left him almost speechless.

"Damn, it looks like the battle is already over," said Hudson, as Tory weaved through the maze of burning hulks of metal; the remains of dozens of CET warships.

"It's not over yet," replied Tory, "there's still a sizeable CET fleet forming a blockade ahead. But it looks almost comically pointless in the face of what's coming."

Hudson peered further out into space and saw the giant shape of Goliath approaching. Straight away, he felt his gut tighten and pulse quicken, as if he'd just been confronted by a rattlesnake or a hungry wolf. He breathed deeply and slowly, before looking ahead of the great ship. Between Goliath and the Orion was a swarm of CET vessels; enough to decimate an entire planet. However, Tory was right – pitted against Goliath, it looked as futile as trying to catch a bullet with a spider's web.

"There are just under three hundred CET ships still in the taskforce," Tory continued, checking her navigation scanner. "The ones that were destroyed seem to have been smashed apart, rather than destroyed with any kind of projectile or energy weapon."

"Seed ships," said Hudson, recognizing the modus operandi of Goliath's minions. Concerned they may also be in danger of attack from the arrow-like ships, Hudson quickly checked his navigation scanner, but he couldn't see any of the vessels nearby. "But it they were attacked by seed drones, where are they all now? Has the CET fleet managed to destroy them?"

Tory scowled and shook her head, "I don't think so..." she replied, ominously. "I'm reading several clusters of smaller ships ahead of Goliath." She glanced at Hudson, still appearing confused. "It's almost as if they're about to collide with each other. But beyond them, I can't get any reliable readings. Whatever is interfering with the comms systems is kicking the crap out of the long-range scanners too."

Hudson also checked the readings, but he didn't understand them either. "None of it matters unless Morphus gets here soon in that Revocater," he said, starting to feel panicky. "Where the hell is that damn alien, anyway?"

Suddenly, the communications console flashed up an incoming message alert. Hudson rushed to check it, and saw that it was coming from one of the CET heavy destroyers. The signal was weak, but just enough to cut through the interference.

"This could be Trent," said Hudson, feeling a brief swell of hope stir inside him. He pulled on his headset, and flipped open the channel. "This is Captain Powell on the Orion. Is that you, Commodore?"

The channel crackled and fizzed like an old a.m. radio, before Trent's familiar voice came back. "It's good to hear your voice, Captain. Did you have any luck recovering the alien crystal?"

"Yes, we have it, but so far there's no sign of our friends," replied Hudson.

"They're on the way," replied Trent. It was like Trent had announced he'd just won the lottery; Hudson couldn't believe that four simple words could bring so much relief and optimism. Even Tory looked vaguely hopeful, instead of her usual, stoic self. "At least I assume it must be them," Trent went on, oblivious to the surge of hope he'd just injected into Hudson's soul, "The ship looks like those that we've seen crashed all over the portal worlds, and it's coming in hot. I have no idea how the thing is moving so fast, but it will be on your scanners imminently."

"Understood, Commodore, we'll rendezvous as soon as we see it," replied Hudson. "Sit tight, and just try to hold them off for as long as you can."

There was distant, urgent chatter in the background on the channel. "Standby, Captain..." said Trent, hurriedly, before he seemed to carry on a conversation with someone on his ship. Hudson left the channel open, and waited anxiously. "We're coming under attack; I must go," Trent eventually said. "We'll try to buy you some time, but in all honesty, our weapons are having barely any effect."

Then, like a bullet train racing towards a station and rapidly coming to a stop, the Revocater sped into view and began to turn towards the battle. Hudson punched the air, and Tory instinctively accelerated towards it.

"Just hang in there, Commodore, the cavalry has arrived!" cried Hudson, "we'll try to bring some heavier firepower into the mix. Powell, out."

The communications channel to Trent's flagship had barely closed, before the light lit up again. This time there was no obvious source. Hudson quickly answered it, and waited. For several seconds there was only static, before a familiar voice spoke.

"Hudson Powell entity, this is Morphus, do you have the crystal?" said Morphus, getting straight to the point.

"Nice to see you again too..." quipped Hudson, buoyed enough by the ship's arrival to let himself feel genuine hope for the first time in days. "You sure as hell know how to make an entrance, Morphus," Hudson continued, joyfully. "And, yes, we have it."

"I am transmitting docking instructions," said Morphus, flatly. The fact the entity did not appear to share Hudson's positivity and enthusiasm concerned him. "You must hurry, Hudson Powell entity. Steer clear of the infiltrators. We will protect you as best we can, as you approach." Then the channel went dead, leaving Hudson a little shell shocked.

"If I didn't know any better, I'd say that thing was scared," said Tory, inputting the new waypoint that Morphus had transmitted into the computer and immediately adjusting course.

"I wonder what it meant by 'steer clear of the infiltrators'?" said Hudson, activating the enhanced weapons systems on the Orion.

"I hope we don't have to find out,' said Tory, pushing the Orion as hard as she could towards the Revocater. "But whatever they are, I'd certainly feel a lot safer inside that big ship than out here in this tin can."

Both of their consoles chimed an alert at the same time. Tory scanned the new data, then quickly turned to Hudson. "We've got incoming!"

Hudson grabbed the weapons controls, and tightened his harness. "I'm on it, just line them up and I'll do the rest."

But Tory shook her head, "I don't think our augmented weapons will be much help this time."

Hudson was about to question why, when he looked up to see five diamond-shaped vessels advancing into the CET fleet. They were like super-sized versions of the seed ships, and while they were nowhere near the size of Goliath or the Revocater, each was double the volume of even Trent's flagship heavy destroyer.

"I'm guessing we've found our infiltrators," said Hudson, as one of the diamond-shaped ships opened fire into the fleet. A beam of energy burst out from the tip of the diamond, cutting a channel straight through one of the cruisers. The stricken vessel flew apart, as if it had been sliced in two by a giant samurai sword. The other infiltrators then attacked, taking out six more CET warships in a matter of seconds.

"The fleet won't last long at this rate!" cried Hudson, returning fire with the Orion's advanced weapons. His shot raked across the side of the closest infiltrator, dealing substantial damage, but it wasn't enough to put it out of commission.

"Hang on!" shouted Tory, as she maneuvered the Orion away from the diamond tip of the infiltrator. The alien vessel retaliated, and the focused column of energy clipped the aft section of the Orion, scoring a narrow furrow across the hull.

Damage indicators lit up on Hudson's panel for the first time since Morphus had radically upgraded its systems. "We won't last long going toe-to-toe with these things, either," said Hudson, noticing that the damage was more significant than he'd expected.

A barrage of cannon fire then erupted from the CET fleet, concentrated onto a single infiltrator. Hudson guessed that perhaps thirty or more ships had focused their weapons onto the alien, but the result was barely more devastating than the Orion had achieved on its own.

"Break off and head for the Revocater," said Hudson, landing a second volley of energy bolts onto another advancing infiltrator. However, as with their first attack, the damage wasn't substantial enough to disable it. "These things are just too strong, and I wouldn't like to test the Orion's armor against a direct hit from their weapons. This ship may be tough, but I don't fancy finding out just how tough it is."

Suddenly, the Orion was hit and thrown into a violent spin. Consoles blew out to the side and rear in the cockpit, and alarms began to blare.

"You had to say it, didn't you!" yelled Tory, as she fought the controls, trying to get the ship back on course.

Hudson checked the damage readout. They had lost pressure in the entire rear section of the ship, but by some miracle the drive systems were still online and they were still flying.

"We've got a hull breach, and damage to a dozen secondary systems," Hudson shouted back. "I don't know how, but we're still in one piece."

Tory wrestled the ship back on course to the Revocater, but it was squirreling around like a rear-wheel drive car on ice. "The way this thing is flying, I actually think we might be missing a few pieces," she replied. Hudson could see the strain in her face and muscles as she battled with the ship. She then glanced down to the navigation scanner and added, "Three of those infiltrators are on us. I don't think we can outrun them."

Hudson pulled the communications console towards him and frantically tried to raise the Revocater, but he couldn't recall the channel Morphus had used. Eventually, he just opened every frequency he could, and broadcast in the clear. "Morphus, we're hit, we need some covering fire!" he called into the microphone. "Morphus, can you hear me?" Hudson yelled, but still there was no reply. Cannon shells detonated ahead of them, as missed shots from the CET fleet flew past. "Morphus, we need you; we're not going to make it!"

Suddenly the blackness of space ahead of them was lit up by hundreds of flashes of energy, all erupting from the Revocater's titanic hull. They raced past the Orion, so close that Hudson was sure some of them grazed their armor. Then the cockpit was bathed in a brilliant white light, filtering in from behind them, and the three pursuing chevrons on the navigation scanner blinked out.

"I don't know if you can hear me, but thanks, Morphus..." said Hudson, before blowing out a sigh and slumping back in his seat.

Tory continued to maneuver the Orion towards their target position on the Revocater's hull, and saw an opening start to appear. A section of the hull towards the front quarter was lowering, like an elevator on an aircraft carrier. Tory positioned the ship over the hole and turned back towards the battle. A black swarm seemed to emerge from Goliath, and head towards the CET fleet, as the great ship sailed on towards Earth.

"I don't like the look of that one bit," said Hudson, as Tory started the delicate maneuver of descending inside the Revocater. He checked the navigation scanner, and saw hundreds of new contacts. "Goliath has launched a damn horde of those seed ships, and a ton of new contacts that I can't even identify," Hudson added, as the front wave of the swarm began to rip through the CET fleet. He glanced at the navigation scanner, then over at Tory. "Make this quick, Trent is down to less than two hundred ships, and dozens of those smaller black dots are coming at us like bullets!"

Tory shot Hudson a dirty look, "I'm going as fast as I can. This isn't as easy as it looks!"

Ten more CET warships had been destroyed, and the swarm was getting closer to them. The space ahead was again lit up by bolts of energy lashing out from the Revocater. However, despite the ferocious onslaught that destroyed dozens of alien vessels in a single strike, some of the smaller enemy ships still slipped through. Hudson watched as the arrow-shaped attackers then thudded into the hull of the enormous ship, impaling themselves in the Revocater like darts sinking into a mighty tree trunk. For the first time, Hudson noticed that the Revocater seemed to have already suffered damage in several places, and now the smaller alien machines were using these openings in an attempt to burrow inside.

"We might have company after we land," said Hudson, as the cockpit dipped below the surface of the Revocater's hull. The opening above them then closed sharply, but they continued to descend into the gut of the alien hulk.

"Somehow, I don't think my .44-40 cartridges are going to be much use against whatever those things were," said Tory.

Then there was a solid thump as the Orion touched down. Tory shut down the engines, unclipped her harness and jumped up, before unhooking the Winchester from over the seat back.

"I thought you said that old relic wouldn't be much use?" said Hudson, jumping up beside her. He then grabbed the rucksack, containing the crystal recombination device, and all of the crystal fragments, and slung it on.

"Only one way to find out..." replied Tory, before hitting the door release. A blast of cool air washed over them as the pressure equalized between the cabin, and their new, alien location.

"I guess I should have probably checked to see if there was atmosphere outside first, huh?" said Tory, with a fatalistic air.

"That might have been a good idea," replied Hudson, trying not to come across as overly condescending. "But since we're not dead, let's head out."

They passed through the corridor connecting the cockpit to the living space, then immediately understood the reason for the ship's erratic maneuvering. There was a column sliced straight through the hull, from top to bottom, cutting directly through the semi-circular couch.

"Shit, Liberty's going to kill me for that," said Hudson, rubbing the back of his neck, awkwardly.

"I think she's fairly low down on the list in terms of people or things that want us dead," said Tory, moving past Hudson.

"I'm not so sure," muttered Hudson, following behind, while trying to ignore the substantial damage to Liberty's pride and joy.

The rear ramp lowered and they both stepped out into the space Morphus had guided them to. It was pitch black, save for the illumination provided from the Orion.

"What now?" asked Hudson, wondering how they were supposed to navigate inside the massive ship in total darkness. Then, as if on cue, a pathway of light illuminated in front of them, leading deeper inside the vessel, like the mysterious yellow brick road.

"I guess we go that way?" shrugged Tory.

"It's funny, I thought the wreck on Brahms Three would be our last relic hunt," mused Hudson. "But here we are again."

Tory shook her head. "This brute isn't a relic yet, not like those other smashed-up old hulks," she said, looking around the chamber. "And it'll stay that way, so long as we don't fail."

CHAPTER 27

With more than a little reluctance, Hudson stepped onto the illuminated pathway that had appeared inside the Revocater, but then the distant clatter and scrape of metal against metal caused him to halt. It was a percussive sound, as if the deck and walls were being rapidly struck with metal bars.

"Hudson Powell and Tory Bellona entities, be aware that there are seed drones approaching your position," came the voice of Morphus, echoing around the chamber.

"Seed drones? What the hell are seed drones?" Hudson called back, but he was then distracted by a glowing alien metal pillar that was rising up out of the deck ahead of him.

"They once helped to transform dead worlds into ones capable of harboring corporeal life," replied Morphus, as Hudson and Tory approached the pillar. "Now they serve Goliath's destructive will."

It was a typically enigmatic, if not entirely unhelpful response from Morphus, thought Hudson. However, the mystery of the seed drones had taken a back seat to the new mystery of what the pillar was. Hudson inspected it more closely, and discovered a drawer at the front. He pulled it out to reveal two large boxes. Glancing at Tory, who looked similarly intrigued, he then flipped open the lid of one of them, and was astonished to see that it was filled with ammunition.

"I do not have the resources to augment your bodies to be more combat-efficient," Morphus continued, "but this ammunition should allow your existing weapons to penetrate the seed drones' armor."

Tory picked up one of the cartridges, and stared at it with bemusement. "I don't get it. Aside from the glowing tip, this looks like a regular .44-40."

Hudson opened the other box, and discovered that it contained ammunition for his pistol. It was identical to what he already carried, save for the same luminous tip.

The floor of the chamber then shook, forcing Hudson to grab the pillar to steady himself. The metallic, clattering noises were also growing louder, but Hudson couldn't place where they were coming from. It felt like a scene out of a horror movie, with strange monsters lurking in the darkness, waiting to attack.

"You must hurry," said Morphus, suddenly more urgent. "I will send more help if I can."

Hudson glanced at Tory and let out an anxious sigh, before grabbing a fistful of bullets. "Alien ammo is better than nothing," he said, as he hurriedly began to reload his pistol.

Tory also emptied the Winchester and loaded the new cartridges, before also reloading her six-shooter. Whether due to her greater experience with weapons, or her iron nerves, Tory had reloaded both firearms and exchanged the regular .44-40s in her ammo holder and pouches, by the time Hudson had finished with his pistol. All the while, the percussive, metallic thuds surrounding them grew louder. The eerie noises even seemed to be getting to Tory.

Hudson finished reloading his spare magazine when a huge contraption on spidery, metal legs like scythes crashed into the chamber from above. It landed with a deafening thud about ten meters from the pillar, and began to clatter towards them.

"Shit, what the hell is that?!" Hudson yelled, as the machine's arrow-shaped body angled downwards, as if it were peering straight at them. He had never been particularly afraid of spiders, but this mechanized arachnid struck terror into his heart like nothing he'd ever seen before.

"I'm guessing that's a seed drone!" said Tory, cocking the Winchester. She then fired five shots in rapid succession straight into the main body of the machine. Each round penetrated through its metal shell, leaving a glowing, circular hole, as if the metal had been melted through. The seed drone staggered forward, then its legs gave way, splaying out underneath it.

"Well, whatever these alien rounds are made of, they work," said Tory. She grabbed five more cartridges from the box in the pillar, which seemed to have replenished itself, and reloaded.

The chamber shuddered again, this time more gently. It felt like the aftershock of an earthquake. Hudson remembered that there were at least two more infiltrators outside, assuming Goliath hadn't launched more. If the CET fleet had been eliminated, then the full focus of the alien armada would now be on the Revocater.

"Let's go, before more of those things find us," said Hudson, slapping the magazine of glowing ammo into his pistol.

Tory moved out ahead, keeping the Winchester cocked and ready. The illuminated pathway advanced ahead of them, guiding them through the maze-like interior of the Revocater. The shudders and shimmies were also growing heavier and more frequent, and the ominous sound of metal clacking on metal was again creeping closer.

Tory moved out in the lead as the corridor narrowed, and pushed through into another large chamber. Hudson immediately recognized the hexagonal central mass and hourglass-shaped conduits from the crashed Revocater on Brahms Three.

"This is the place," said Hudson, feeling excitement building inside him. "It's just like in the wreck on Brahms Three. The navigation hub should be through that far wall, on the other side of this chamber."

Tory started moving through the room, but she'd made it only a couple of paces, before a seed drone scurried out of a corridor at the far end. Suddenly, another two entered from the opposite corridor, and all three began cutting into the wall with focused, laser-like tools. Seconds later, two more drones scuttled down from the opening above the large hexagonal mass.

"I'm glad I picked up plenty of ammo..." said Tory, tracking the closest seed drone as it dropped down onto the metal deck. Its scythe-like legs thudded against the floor, before it scraped its way towards them.

Hudson opened fire first with the pistol, hitting the drone's arrow-shaped mass. The rounds pierced through, but his pistol lacked the penetrative power of Tory's Winchester, and it took almost his entire magazine to put the machine down.

While Hudson was firing, Tory engaged the second drone that had clambered down from the hexagonal central mass. The alien contraption was quickly incapacitated with four tightly-grouped shots, and crashed to the deck in a contorted heap.

Suddenly, Hudson heard the scrape of metal behind him, and he spun around to see another seed drone dragging itself through the opening. He immediately fired, but on the third shot he heard the tell-tale click of an empty chamber.

"Shit, Tory, I need to reload!" he cried, scrambling away from the drone as he released the magazine and fumbled for another.

Tory turned and crouched to one knee, cocking and firing twice before the drone lashed out with its long leg. Tory was flung towards the center of the room, and the Winchester spiraled from her grasp.

Hudson cried out after her, before slapping the second magazine into the pistol. The drone advanced, but Hudson ducked underneath its leg, narrowly avoiding being impaled. Aiming directly into the machine's body, he squeezed the trigger as fast as he could, unloading five rounds at point-blank range. The seed drone staggered backwards, and Hudson dived out from underneath it, a split-second before the drone crashed to the ground.

Hudson ran over to Tory, who was slowly pushing herself upright. Her armored jacket had been slashed open, and Hudson could see blood soaking into her tank top around her stomach.

"I'm fine, it's not deep," said Tory, climbing up onto her knees, and noticing the worried look on Hudson's face.

Hudson helped Tory to stand and they both turned to face the remaining three seed drones. However, they seemed to be ignoring them, and focused on cutting through the end wall with their laser-like weapons.

"We can't let those things get inside the navigation hub," said Hudson tightening his grip on the pistol.

Tory nodded and took off the tattered remains of her armored jacket, before throwing it down and recovering the Winchester rifle from the deck. "I don't know about you, but I've already had enough of these spiky bastards," she growled, sliding more rounds into the rifle.

Hudson checked his magazine; he only had three rounds left. "I don't disagree, but I only have a few more shots," he said, slapping the magazine back into the weapon. "I'm only going to be able to piss one of them off before I'm out."

Tory drew her six shooter and held it out to Hudson, "Here, this will put at least one of them down," she said, as Hudson took it. "Leave the other two to me."

Hudson holstered the pistol and switched the six-shooter to his right hand. It felt a lot heavier, and somehow more lethal, even without the benefit of alien-tipped rounds.

"Just one thing," added Tory, as she got ready to advance. "Lose that, or break it, and we're going to have a serious falling out..."

Hudson huffed a laugh, "Don't worry, I know you love this thing more than me," he said. Then he realized his slip, and stammered, "Not that you love me, of course, I'm not saying that at all..."

Tory smiled and quickly pecked him on the cheek. "Shut up, already, will you?"

Hudson did as he was ordered, grateful that Tory's reaction had spared him more blushes. However, he couldn't help notice that she hadn't contradicted him, either.

"Let's do this," said Tory, pacing towards the seed drones by the end wall, and snapping Hudson out of his daydream.

Hudson cocked the antique weapon and moved up alongside her. The three drones still continued to cut into the wall, as if they didn't see them as a threat.

"I think we need to get their attention," said Tory, aiming and firing three shots at the drone in the center. Its legs splayed out and it crashed to the deck, immediately causing the other two to stop, and spin around.

"There are only two to go," said Hudson. "You take the one on the left, I'll take the one on the right."

Hudson aimed, but then two more drones scuttled inside the room from the corridors on the side walls.

"Shit…" said Hudson, realizing he'd again spoken too soon.

Then the sound of metal clacking against metal reverberated down the chamber from the rear, and another drone entered behind them.

"Back up!" said Tory, who was already stepping away from the end wall. "We can use the central mass as cover."

Hudson also started to pace away from the drones, but now all four were slowly stalking them. "Morphus, if ever you were going to help us out, now is the time!" he shouted out into the air.

They reached the hexagonal mass and pressed their backs against it. Tory crouched and took aim. "I think we're on our own," she said. "Keep your groupings tight. If we're lucky, two or three shots should be enough."

Hudson nodded, and took several deep breaths. His hand was already shaking so much he doubted he could get three shots on target, never mind in a tight grouping. He was about to fire his first round when there was a deep, resonant thud from the far wall. It sounded as though a huge bolt had just slid open in a vault. The seed drones stopped, and looked back as the center of the wall began to open up, like an iris. Hudson and Tory stood up, to get a clearer view of what was beyond, before they saw someone walking out of the iris towards them.

"Is it Morphus?" asked Tory, as the figure cleared the threshold and entered the room.

Hudson smiled, and shook his head. "No, it's not Morphus," he said, recognizing her purposeful walk immediately. "That's Liberty."

"What's she got in her hands?" asked Tory, noticing the two shimmering staffs in Liberty's grasp. "And why the hell are her arms glowing?"

Liberty punched the tonfa towards Hudson, and he ducked instinctively as a bolt of energy flashed past. Turning behind, he saw the seed drone that had entered from the rear collapse to the deck. There was a hole cut directly through its central mass, as if Liberty had bored into it with an enormous drill. He spun back to Liberty with the intention of asking how she'd done it, but his mouth just hung open.

"Well, don't just stand there!" shouted Liberty, throwing her arms out wide. "Shoot the damn things!"

Tory reacted before Hudson could regain his senses, shooting the drone on her far left four times and putting it down. Liberty darted forward and attacked the drone nearest to her, unleashing whip-like talons of energy with each flourish of the glowing tonfas. The machine was split in half, as if struck with an enormous cleaver.

Another seed drone advanced on Liberty, but Hudson was ready this time. He pulled the trigger of the six-shooter and hit the drone's rear quarter, causing the machine to stumble and falter. Hudson cocked the six shooter and fired twice more, striking first to the drone's central mass, before taking one of the scythe-like legs clean off. Liberty moved in and finished off the machine in another impressive display with her strange alien weapons.

A single drone remained. Its arrow-like body jolted from Liberty to Hudson and then to Tory, as if it were unsure of who posed the greatest threat to it. It then darted for Tory, but the crack of the Winchester stopped it in its tracks. Hudson fired again, this time hitting the machine dead center, before Liberty moved in, punching the tonfa towards the drone and finishing it cleanly.

Hudson was left breathless and shaky, hardly believing that they'd survived the onslaught. He peered around the chamber, but other than the smoldering remains of the seed drones, and themselves, it was clear. He turned back, but was almost knocked off his feet as Liberty flung herself at him, throwing her arms around his neck.

"You made it!" she cried, beaming a smile at him.

"Apparently, so did you," replied Hudson, smiling back at her. Then he noticed the glowing weapons that were still wrapped around his neck. "Though you appear to have found a couple of new alien artefacts since we were last together?"

"Long story..." said Liberty, stepping back, and nodding respectfully towards Tory, who returned the gesture, "and we're short on time. Do you have the crystal?"

Hudson took the rucksack off his back and held it out to her. "Two parts of an alien crystal, a recombination chamber, and a whole bunch of fragments," he said. "I sure as hell hope that Morphus knows what to do with it."

Liberty slid the tonfas through her belt. "I hope so too," she said, more somberly, "because the CET fleet is all but gone, and we only have a few minutes before Goliath reaches Earth."

Hudson nodded, "If that ship is half as smart as Morphus says it is, then this crystal should certainly get its attention."

Liberty took the rucksack from Hudson, and peered inside. The fragments of crystals were glowing, like her augmentations. She smiled, and her own eyes took on a steelier edge. "It's time we kicked this bully where it really hurts."

CHAPTER 28

Hudson and Tory followed Liberty through the iris-like opening in the wall and into the Revocater's navigation hub. The iris then closed behind them, once again sealing off the titanic vessel's effective command center from any other seed drones that may have made it inside. All three then hurried to the far side of the navigation hub, and found Morphus standing in front of two wildly different starship flight decks.

On the left, Hudson immediately recognized the layout as being the same as that of the Orion. However, the consoles on the right were a wild juxtaposition of modern, high-end cockpit design, with something straight out of the Dam Busters. He watched as the ball turret rotated rapidly in midair, and saw the bolts of energy race out into space all around them. Then Hudson noticed who was controlling the turret, and had to do a double-take. He turned to Liberty, full of questions.

"Is that Tobin or have I finally lost my marbles?" Hudson asked, a little louder than he'd planned.

"Hey, Hudson," replied Tobin from the turret. "You'll have to excuse me if I don't get up," he added, while destroying several seed drones that were attempting to ram the Revocater.

Hudson turned back to Tobin, then to Liberty again, but with all of the questions fighting for precedence, he was unable to articulate any of them.

"He was almost killed by a seed drone while we were fighting on the surface of the Corporeals' home world," Liberty began, anticipating what Hudson might want to know. "Morphus healed him with that strange glowy metal, and now he's basically the Revocater's gunner, in that recreation of a B17 Sperry ball turret."

"Makes perfect sense to me," interrupted Tory, placing her hand underneath Hudson's chin and gently closing his gaping mouth. Then Tory turned to Morphus. "So, alien lady, what do we do with these crystals?"

Liberty handed the rucksack to Morphus, and the entity removed the recombination device, before examining the crystal shards and fragments.

"This will be sufficient to recombine a crystal," the entity said, and Hudson heard everyone in the room let out a collective sigh of relief. However,

Morphus did not allow any time for celebrations. "We must be ready the moment the crystal chamber comes online," it added, with a cautionary tone. "Goliath knows that a single Revocater cannot defeat it. It has toyed with us until now, intent on tormenting my programming for as long as possible. But once it detects the crystal, the great ship will unleash the full extent of its power on this ship."

A pillar then rose up between the two stations, and Morphus placed the recombination device on top. It sank into the alien metal and Hudson watched through a transparent window as the two objects blended into a seamless whole. Four tubes connected the device to the pillar, just as Hudson had found it on the other Revocater. Morphus then placed the crystal shards on top, and Hudson watched as they also sank into the metal. A few seconds later, they were visible through the window. Hudson took a deep breath and let it out slowly. They were finally ready, he realized.

"Liberty, please set a collision course with Goliath," said Morphus, turning to the Revocater's augmented human pilot.

Liberty's eyebrows shot up on her forehead. "You want me to do what now with Goliath?" she replied, in the manner that people often ask others to repeat instructions that seem patently insane.

"I want you to set a collision course with Goliath," answered Morphus, restating its precise instruction. However, the disturbed look on Liberty's face encouraged the alien to elaborate on its reasons. "At the moment, Goliath is content to methodically whittle this ship down. It wishes to cripple the Revocater, and force us to spectate, safe in the knowledge we cannot stop it," Morphus added. "But if Goliath believes we will ram it, in a last-ditch effort to thwart its victory, it will turn from the planet and confront us."

"And that's what we want?" Hudson cut in. Like Liberty, he was struggling to see the benefit of Morphus' new order.

"I assume you do not want Goliath to remove the planet's core, causing Earth to crumble to dust?" replied Morphus, with a slight eyebrow raise of its own.

Tory laughed, and Liberty and Hudson scowled at her, failing to see the funny side. "What? The alien lady has some sass!" Tory said, shrugging.

"Trust me, Liberty Devan entity," said Morphus. "Time is short."

Liberty shot an uncertain glance at Hudson, but at this point he had to take Morphus on faith. He nodded back to her, and Liberty returned to her station, before turning the Revocater towards Goliath and increasing their speed. Hudson and Tory waited with Morphus, and watched as the recombination chamber began to glow brighter, like the raging furnace of a steam locomotive.

The floor shook again, and Hudson saw the diamond-like shape of an infiltrator swoop past the panoramic view that wrapped around them. Tobin quickly spun the turret after it and destroyed the vessel with a swarm of energy bolts. However, Hudson could see that others were combining from the hundreds of seed drones that were still buzzing around them. There were now fewer than twenty CET vessels left in Trent's once mighty war fleet. In less than an hour, Goliath had almost wiped out Earth's entire defenses.

Suddenly there was a thud from the far side of the chamber, followed by several more sharp, metallic strikes. Hudson and Tory exchanged nervous glances and turned to Morphus.

"Seed drones are attempting to break through," the entity explained. "I have used the last of my available resources to seal off the engine and reactor chambers, to prevent the drones from detonating inside and crippling the Revocater." A second pillar rose up behind Morphus, and Hudson saw that it again contained the glowing alien ammunition. "I must now focus my energy on confronting Goliath," Morphus added, in its usual, highly understated manner. "Please assist me by holding off any seed drones that manage to break through."

Hudson and Tory met each other's eyes briefly, then began hastily reloading their weapons. Though Morphus had made its request sound no more urgent than an invitation to answer the door, both of them knew the consequences should the seed drones get inside and destroy the crystal chamber, or even Morphus itself.

Tory finished pushing the alien .44-40s into the six-shooter, and closed the cylinder. "Take this again," she said, holding the six-shooter out to Hudson. "You'll need more firepower than that little pistol can deliver."

Hudson nodded and took the revolver. "I don't imagine the people who made these weapons thought that this would be the frontier they'd be used in."

Tory finished sliding the last round into the Winchester and cocked it. "No, but this time the stakes are far higher than the Wild West," said Tory. "Let's just hope this isn't our last stand."

Suddenly, the intense light from the hexagonal pillar diminished. Hudson glanced back and saw that a fully-formed crystal was now visible inside it, and was glowing vividly. Then he heard another powerful, low thrum harmonize with the sound of the Revocater's immense reactors.

"Morphus..." Liberty called out. The distress in her voice caused Hudson to look up at the screen. The reason for Liberty's concern was immediately obvious – Goliath had turned towards them, and was closing rapidly.

"It's coming straight at us," Liberty continued, breathlessly, "and the Shaak radiation levels are beginning to climb!"

"Reduce speed and stand by," said Morphus, before the entity sank into its pod.

"Stand by for what?!" cried Liberty, slowing the mighty Revocater so that they now sat toe-to-toe with the great ship, but Morphus had already disappeared and merged with the Revocater. "Damn, I wish it would stop doing that!" cried Liberty, turning back to the view outside, which was now utterly consumed by the vast form of Goliath.

The new sound that had begun when the crystal was recombined now overtook even the thrum of the Revocater's reactors. The entire crystal chamber and hexagonal pillar was now glowing, as if it was white hot, but strangely Hudson could still look at it without hurting his eyes.

"Shaak radiation levels just doubled!" cried Liberty. "And that was double a level that was already off the chart..." Hudson ran to her side and read the instruments.

"Wait, some of the Shaak build-up is coming from us," said Hudson. Then looked up at Goliath on the screen, stalking them as if they were a wounded animal. "It's not just Goliath that's trying to cast a portal; Morphus is too!"

Tory rushed up beside Hudson, and they all watched as the two titanic vessels prepared to throw each other across the galaxy. Two massive swirling vortices of energy began to form between the rival vessels, pushing against each other like giant sumo wrestlers. The thrum inside the navigation hub rose to a near-deafening roar, and it seemed like the entire frame of the Revocater twisted and groaned under the immense strain. The standoff continued for several more seconds, neither one of the two mighty ships giving an inch, but then the conjoined vortices began to slowly creep back towards them. The titanic frame of the Revocater began to buckle, like a soda can slowly being crushed.

"Morphus, what's happening?" shouted Hudson, peering around the chamber for any sign of the entity.

"We're losing, that's what is happening," said Tory, pensively.

Hudson met Tory's eyes for a moment, and he could see that she sensed defeat. Peering back outside, it was now clear that Goliath was pushing the portals back towards the Revocater. The great ship was overcoming Morphus with sheer, brute strength.

"No, we can't have come this far only to lose now!" cried Hudson, thumping the console. Then he turned to the pod that Morphus had sunk into and stared down into it. "Morphus, there must be something more we can do. Anything!"

There was a moment's silence, like the wait for the executioner's axe to fall, before Morphus' voice filled the chamber.

"There is only one option remaining," it said, its voice sounding strained and weak. "You must all leave. To defeat Goliath, I must give all this vessel has, and more. For humanity to live, I must die."

CHAPTER 29

Morphus' shock announcement hit Hudson like a hammer strike to the head. For several seconds he just stood over the alien entity's pod, completely lost for words. He turned to the others for inspiration, but each of their faces wore the same stupefied expression as his.

The words continued to echo around Hudson's mind. Morphus had literally taken a bullet for him on New Providence station, and during their time together he'd developed a genuine fondness for the entity's curious ways. It wasn't just a machine; it was a friend, and just as much a part of the crew as Liberty, Tory and Tobin.

"Morphus' you can't sacrifice yourself to save us, not again!" said Liberty, as she and the others joined Hudson beside the entity's pod, "There must be another way."

"There is not."

The voice came from the center of the chamber. They all turned to see Morphus standing there, in the female form they had grown accustomed to. Hudson and the others hurried over to Morphus, before Hudson noticed that it was still connected to the deck, as if its boots were fused to it.

"Come on, you have to give us another option," said Hudson, echoing Liberty's views. "You can't just throw your life away like this."

The entity returned a warm and reassuring smile, and in that moment, Hudson realized that Morphus was the most human it had ever looked.

"This is my function, Hudson Powell entity," said Morphus, calmly. "I was created specifically to protect corporeal life."

Hudson shook his head. "Maybe that's how they built you, but you're more than that to us," he hit back. "You're not expendable, Morphus."

The vibrations through the deck were growing stronger, and Hudson could also see that sections of the far wall were close to being cut through by the seed drones outside. They were out of time, and out of options. Despite their protestations, Hudson knew Morphus was right.

"I am the last Revocater," said Morphus, firmly. "You are the last sentient corporeal species in the galaxy. I am one – you are many. It is that simple."

"To hell with that," said Liberty, with matching determination. "You have just as much right to exist as we do. There must be another way!"

Morphus shook its head, solemnly. "I can only hold off Goliath's portal for a few more minutes," it said, as parts of its body destabilized and turned to liquid gold. "You must leave. You must survive. Otherwise, I will have failed again."

A chunk of the far wall fell through into the navigation hub, and the scythe-like leg of a seed drone poked through.

"I thank you for your companionship," said Morphus, as its form began to reintegrate with the ship. "Do not be sad."

Liberty reached out and held the alien entity's hands, refusing to let it go. "Come with us, please..." she pleaded, but Morphus continued to melt away.

"You must go, Liberty..." said Morphus, weakly, before its female form became an anonymous mass of shimmering gold. The alien metal flowed through Liberty's hands, and it was gone.

Hudson's head dropped low. He knew Morphus still existed inside the ship, but it still felt like a death had just occurred. However, there was no time to grieve – the swirling purple vortices were creeping closer, and if they reached the Revocater, they would be thrown across the galaxy, and lost forever. Morphus – as usual – had been correct. They had to leave, immediately.

"We have to get back to the Orion," Hudson shouted, stuffing his jacket pocket with additional ammo, "come on, let's move!" Liberty was on her knees, pressing her hands to the spot where Morphus had vanished. Hudson dropped down beside her, and met her eyes. "Mourn Morphus later, Liberty. If we don't go now, there won't be any of us left to remember her."

"You called it 'her'," said Liberty, managing a feeble smile.

"Well, Morphus is a damn sight more human than most humans I've known," replied Hudson, not even realizing his slip. Then he spoke more determinedly again, and held out his hand. "Come on, Liberty; while we still have time..."

Liberty took Hudson's hand, and together they rose up. Checking on the others, Hudson saw that Tory was already aiming the Winchester at the door, standing guard while the others gathered their senses.

Hudson then glanced at Tobin and saw that he wasn't armed. "Here, you'll need this," he said, offering Tobin his pistol.

Tobin smiled and waved Hudson off. "Thanks, but I already have one of my own," he said, lifting up his right arm. His skin suddenly became golden, like Morphus, and his hand turned to a glowing, amorphous mass. When the luster had died down, Hudson saw a shimmering pistol in Tobin's hand. "My recent augmentations have some advantages," Tobin added, still smiling.

"That's a pretty nice trick," said Tory, looking genuinely impressed. "I have an idea," she added, before pointing to Tobin and then Liberty. "How about you two cyborg super soldiers go first?"

Suddenly, the end wall collapsed inwards, and three seed drones pulled themselves inside the navigation hub. Tobin reacted even more rapidly than Tory, immediately shooting the first with his alien weapon. The blast burned a hole straight through the drone's triangular central mass, and it dropped to the deck, as if Tobin had just flipped an off switch.

Liberty drew the alien tonfas from her belt and charged at the other two. She lashed out with the whip-like enhancements that emanated from the ends of the martial-arts weapons, hitting both in quick succession. Within seconds, the seed drones all lay destroyed on the ground.

"I second Tory's plan," said Hudson, feeling slightly overwhelmed by the ferocious display of aggression from the young duo. "You two should definitely go first..."

Liberty and Tobin smiled at each other, then moved out ahead into the corridor. Hudson and Tory followed, and again they saw the illuminated pathway.

"Thank you, Morphus..." said Hudson, glad of the entity's continued assistance. Then he called out, "Just follow the lights; they'll lead us back to the Orion!"

Suddenly the hole in the wall that had been cut out by the seed drones was sealed by a curtain of glowing metal. Morphus was using all the strength it had remaining to give them the opportunity to escape. Hudson knew it would act true to its function, until the very last.

Liberty and Tobin again led the group, as another seed drone clattered out of an adjacent corridor to confront them. Tobin shot it without hesitation and pressed on, with Liberty at his side. The pair had barely made it ten meters, before the ceiling of the corridor suddenly collapsed in behind them. Three seed drones dropped down, separating Hudson and Tory from Liberty and Tobin.

Tory wasted no time, dispatching the closest alien machine with two precisely-aimed shots from the Winchester. Hudson cocked the six-shooter and fired, hitting the next one in its body. However, the drone still advanced, and Hudson was forced to duck as it swung its scythe-like leg towards his head. The sharp metal dug into the corridor wall, and was momentarily stuck, giving Hudson just enough time to pull back the hammer again and fire. A shower of sparks burst out from the triangular body, and the seed drone stopped moving.

With barely a second to breathe, another seed drone smashed through the carcass of its fallen companion, knocking Hudson to his back. It raised its bladed leg, ready to impale Hudson through the heart, and he tried to pull back the hammer again, but fumbled. The metal leg dropped, and he threw out his hands, desperately trying to fend it away, but instead of stabbing through his flesh, the sharp metal impaled into the deck, inches from his head. He looked up and saw Liberty, poised underneath the drone. She had struck the leg away at the last moment, and was now following up with another sequence of strikes from the glowing tonfas. Each blow smashed off one of the machine's metal limbs, as if they were nothing more substantial than balsawood.

Hudson scrambled away, as the drone slumped down across the corridor wall, crackling and fizzing with residual energy.

"I'm getting really tired of these things..." said Hudson, as Liberty helped him up.

"You and me both," replied Liberty, glancing ahead to check on Tobin, "but we've not seen the last of them yet."

Hudson then saw Tory rapidly firing at a new group of seed drones that were approaching from the rear. "Try to clear a path to the Orion," Hudson said, turning back to Liberty. "I'll get Tory."

Liberty cocked her head, "Remember when I said she'd be the death of you?"

"What can I say? I'm a glutton for punishment," replied Hudson, before slapping Liberty on the shoulder. "Now go do your ninja, Kung-Fu stick thing." Liberty smiled and shook her head, before running along the corridor to assist Tobin.

Hudson ran in the opposite direction and fired two of the six-shooter's three remaining rounds at one of the pursuing drones. The machine fell, and the crack of Tory's Winchester soon finished off the last two. The corridor behind them was finally clear.

"Liberty and Tobin are clearing the route ahead," Hudson called over to Tory, as she cocked the rifle again. "We only have a few minutes to get out."

Tory rushed to join Hudson, and together they ran along the corridor, following the illuminated path. Hudson clambered over the broken remains of seed drones that had already fallen victim to the augmented humans, and charged into the chamber where they had landed the Orion. Feeling a swell of relief, Hudson rushed on, but then another seed drone smashed through the deck from below. It clawed itself up, like some sort of hideous mechanical undead spider, and blocked their path.

Tory stepped forward, aimed the Winchester, and fired, but the weapon merely clicked.

"Shit, I'm out!" she cried, scrambling in her pouches for any more of the alien ammo.

Tory was still scrabbling to get her fingers around one of the alien cartridges when the seed drone charged at them. Without thinking, Hudson clicked back the hammer of the six-shooter and fired. The round penetrated the drone's arrow-shaped body in the dead center, and the machine crumpled to the deck, as if stepped on by a giant boot.

"Hell of a shot!" said Tory, smiling, "though I bet you couldn't do it again."

Hudson shook his head and laughed, "How about we not wait around to find out?"

Clambering over the bodies of more destroyed drones, Hudson and Tory ran up to the Orion. Liberty had already lowered the rear ramp, and she and Tobin were holding off the remaining drones. Hudson hurried inside the ship, while Tory remained outside to lend a hand, using the last few alien cartridges she could find in her many pouches. He reached the living space, then to his horror he remembered the damage the ship had suffered before landing. However, when he reached the semi-circular couch, the self-healing alien alloy had sealed the hull ruptures, leaving just the scar cut through the interior.

"She's still going to kill me when she sees that," Hudson muttered to himself as he winced at the gash cut through the couch, before racing past it and into the cockpit. Waving his arm in front of the console, the Orion's reactor sparked into life and the engines fired.

"We're inside, and the ramp is closed!" shouted Liberty, speaking through the intercom from the cargo hold. "Get us out of here!"

Hudson lifted the Orion off the deck, and aimed the nose towards the next wave of seed drones flooding in. The ship still felt squirrely and out of sorts, but the damage control panel showed they at least had pressure. He activated the weapons systems, and waited for the targeting reticules to lock on.

The door to the cockpit opened and the others all rushed in and strapped into their seats, as Hudson unleased a burst of energy bolts at the drones. The powerful blasts destroyed four machines instantly, and created a shockwave that knocked a dozen others over like skittles.

"Look, the way out is clear!" shouted Tory, peering up through the canopy. Morphus was opening their doorway out into space, giving no more regard for the safety of the Revocater. Hudson knew, just as Morphus had done, that the Revocater would not survive this final battle.

Hudson engaged the ventral thrusters and surged the Orion upwards. His focus was laser-precise, but half way up the long vertical tunnel, a seed drone dropped down onto the ship from outside.

"Damn it, if that thing ruptures the hull, we're done for!" shouted Hudson. The drone's spidery metal legs dug in, and it prepared to activate its cutting beam.

"If ever you were to have a genius moment of inspiration, Hudson, now is the time!" cried Liberty.

"Hang on!" Hudson shouted. He then flipped the Orion over by ninety degrees, and teased the ship closer to the wall of the tunnel. The seed drone was squashed against the surface, but desperately tried to cling on, using its scythe-like legs to bite deeper into the hull. However, the Orion's upgraded alien armor resisted its hold.

"Get off, you spidery asshole!" Hudson yelled, pushing the Orion harder against the wall. The drone's body tore away from its legs, leaving the metal scythes impaled in the hull, like a crown.

"Okay, you're officially a genius!" cried Liberty, slapping the arms of her chair as the Orion blasted out into space.

Hudson put some distance between them and the Revocater, before turning the ship to face the two giant alien vessels. They were still locked in their epic contest, and Goliath was prevailing.

Silence fell over the cockpit as they watched the glow of the Revocater's engines darken. Cracks began to surface in its armor, and glowing golden light bled out. A console in the second seat chimed an alert, and Liberty hurriedly checked it.

"It's a Shaak radiation spike," she said, her voice ragged and fearful. "It's bigger than anything I've ever seen..."

The glow through the Revocater's fractured hull plating grew more intense. The Shaak pulse was now so powerful that it was distorting gravity in the space around the ships, shaking the Orion like it was a raft on turbulent seas. However, whatever it was that Morphus was doing, Hudson could see it was working. The swirling purple vortices were not only pushing back towards Goliath, they were growing larger by the second.

Suddenly, all of the remaining seed ships broke away from their attacks on the fractured remains of the CET armada. Forming up, they raced towards the Revocater, each one impaling itself into the surface. It was like Goliath was trying to deal death by a thousand cuts.

Still no-one spoke as seed ship after seed ship thudded into the Revocater's hull, chipping away at its alien metal like a thousand chisels. The Revocater surged on, glowing more intensely by the second, and still the swirling purple vortices accelerated towards Goliath.

Hudson could almost sense the desperation of the great ship, as hundreds of seed ships reformed into infiltrators. Ten of the diamond-shaped weapons then began to cut into the Revocater's hull, but it was already too late. With one final, immense push, Morphus overpowered Goliath's portal.

Free from any resistance, Morphus' portal raced towards Goliath and enveloped it, like a titanic black hole consuming a star. The great ship began to disappear, as kilometer upon kilometer of its gigantic hull was swallowed by the purple vortex. Then, in a matter of seconds, Goliath was gone.

The second purple vortex also fizzled to nothing, and the gravity distortions ceased. With their master gone, the remaining seed drones and infiltrators all lost power, and began listing in space, like flotsam on the ocean.

"Morphus did it..." said Hudson, speaking in barely more than a whisper. "It's gone."

There was no sense of elation. All eyes were now turned to the last Revocater – to Morphus. The glow from the ship had faded to nothing, and its mighty engines remained dark. Powerless to resist the pull of Earth's gravity, the Revocater sank towards the planet. Not knowing what else to do, Hudson followed it, desperately hoping that the alien entity would regain power and halt its descent, but in his heart, Hudson knew that Morphus was already lost. It had given everything it had to fulfil its function, and now it would come to its end in System 5118208, on the planet it was entrusted to protect, millennia earlier.

Morphus had succeeded. It had saved them all, but the cost had been great.

CHAPTER 30

Ma brought over the next round of drinks from the bar and set the tumblers and beer bottles down on the table. Ma had chosen the venue; a dive bar on Market Street, between 14th and 15th. Even though it wasn't her place, Ma still liked playing host, and seemed perfectly happy and at home serving up the various drinks. Besides Ma, the table was occupied by Hudson, Tory, Liberty, Tobin and Commodore Trent, although he wasn't in uniform, and preferred everyone to call him by his given name, Elias.

It had been just over forty-eight hours since Goliath had been cast through the portal. In that time, the Revocater had fallen through Earth's atmosphere and crashed into the Gulf of the Farallones, along the shoreline of Point Reyes National Seashore, north of San Francisco. Reports had described the titanic ship's descent as a 'controlled crash'. Hudson had no way to know, but he believed that Morphus had used what little life it had left to ensure its own demise did not harm any corporeal life.

Once the Revocater had come to rest, Hudson had landed the Orion on its now fractured hull. Together with Tory, Liberty and Tobin, they had climbed inside the new wreck and found their way to the navigation hub. Hudson had reactivated Morphus once before, and he had desperately hoped he could do it again. However, once inside, they had found the human female form of Morphus sitting in the pilot's seat of the replica VCX-110 cockpit. The entity's eyes were open, staring out at what was now a featureless metal wall. However, the unique, golden glow shining inside them was gone, and whatever life energy Morphus had possessed within its circuits was absent too.

Trent had arrived some hours later; his flagship had been one of only three CET vessels to survive Goliath's onslaught. Three out of five hundred. With his help, and the assistance of the planet-based CET aircraft, they had moved Morphus' body to a secure facility.

Trent had assured Hudson that the entity would not be dissected or experimented on in any way. Hudson had wanted to lay the entity to rest, but Trent had argued that to leave Morphus in the Revocater, or bury it, as he and Liberty had requested, would have merely attracted future hunters. Similarly, the crystal recombination chamber, and the now-fractured remains of the crystal, had also been removed and placed in secure storage.

A Shaak radiation perimeter was quickly established around the wrecked Revocater to ensure nothing else was taken. Even Hudson and the others were scanned before leaving the ship. Trent had apologized profusely for this, but insisted that more research had to be done on the vessel's technology. Humanity had been reckless in its use of the alien relics, and too eager to venture into the stars. Trent wanted to ensure that humanity's reach no longer exceeded its grasp.

"Come on, this is supposed to be a celebration, not a wake," said Ma, spreading the glasses out in front of everyone. "We won, right?"

Liberty was probably the most downcast of them all. "I'm still too angry to be happy," she said, producing confused frowns from the others around the table. She picked up the glass of whiskey and downed it, before noticing the bemused looks on the faces staring back at her. "You know what I mean," she added, with an eye roll.

"If anyone should be angry, it's me," said Ma, before pointing a finger at Tory. "I've still not forgiven you for taking me out of the game, young lady." Tory smiled and held up her hands in surrender. Then Ma leant in closer, and whispered, "Though if you can get me a couple of those silent takedown buzzers, I might let it slide."

Trent coughed. "Such devices are highly illegal on Earth." Ma and Tory sat back, met the Commodore's eyes and held them, both looking distinctly unimpressed. "Though, with so much to do in the aftermath of the invasion, one might potentially overlook such things," Trent swiftly added.

"I'll drink to that," said Ma, raising her glass, before swallowing the contents and wincing. "I've had enough of this crap, already," she added, before ducking under the table and pulling a square bottle out of her bag. She placed it on the table, then proceeded to pour all the other glasses into her empty tumbler.

"I don't think you're allowed to bring your own booze in here," said Tobin, though in truth he had been thoroughly enjoying Ma's eccentricity and hilarious relic hunter anecdotes for the last couple of hours. A bald man who was as wide as he was tall then began to amble over from behind the bar. "See..." said Tobin, pointing at the enormous man, "you're going to get us thrown out."

The bald man arrived and slipped a credit scanner onto the table in front of Ma. She picked it up, but Trent hastily intervened.

"Oh no, please allow me to pay for the drinks," he said, looking embarrassed that Ma had picked up the scanner. "It literally is the very least I can do."

Ma thumbed the scanner, and also held it to her face for an iris scan.

"Damn, Ma, how expensive was that last round?" asked Hudson. Typically, an iris scan was only required for significant transaction amounts.

"This isn't for the drinks," said Ma, as if it should have been obvious. "I've just bought the bar."

Hudson opened his mouth, but not for the first time in the last couple of days, he couldn't suitably articulate what he was thinking.

Tory leaned over the table and took the cork out of the square bottle. "Now that really is a cause for celebration," she said, pouring a healthy measure into each glass.

Hudson looked at the stout, former bar owner, still wearing a slightly stupefied look on his face. "You sold this place to her, just like that?" he asked, trying to understand how such a rapid business transaction could occur.

"Look, pal, I've seen some crazy shit in this town, but giant alien space ships falling out of the sky beats it all," he said, taking the scanner back off Ma. "I'm retiring..." Then he looked back at Ma and said, "I'll bring you all the paperwork after we close," before wandering off again.

Tory slid the square bottle over to Ma, since her glass was full of the previous, inferior spirit. "So, what are you going to call this place?" she asked, raising her tumbler at the former hunter.

Ma caught the bottle and held it up. "I thought I'd call it, 'The Star Scavenger's Rest.' It's got a nice ring to it, don't you think?"

Hudson smiled and raised his glass. "Well, it certainly sounds less like a strip joint than your last bar."

There was a ripple of laughter around the table, then Liberty said, "To the Star Scavenger's Rest. May it be a welcome retreat for weary relic hunters everywhere."

There was a chorus of, 'To the Star Scavenger's Rest', then everyone at the table downed their shots, while Ma swigged directly from the bottle. Tobin and Trent both almost bent double, slapping their chests, while the others looked on and chuckled knowingly.

Suddenly, the door to the bar flung open and a hooded figure marched in. He quickly surveyed the room, saw Hudson and paced over. Within seconds, the figure had pulled out a pistol and aimed it at Hudson. The figure then whipped back his hood, and Logan Griff stood in front of them, his wiry black moustache twitching, angrily.

"Did you think I wouldn't find you, rook?" Griff snarled. "You think you can just sit and drink in a bar, like nothing happened?" Griff was furious, even on the verge of being unhinged. "It doesn't work that way, rook!" Griff continued, tightening his grip on the weapon, "You were never going to beat me. And now, you're finally going to pay."

Hudson picked up his beer and casually took a swig, before he shuffled in his seat to face Griff. "Did you really think we'd forgotten about you?" he said, and instantly Griff's face fell. "Did you really think the CET haven't been tracking your every movement since you killed three of their soldiers?" Hudson cocked an eyebrow, inviting Griff to respond, but for the first time since he'd met him, his former partner was speechless. Hudson sighed, elaborately, and shook his head. "You really are the dumbest ex-RGF cop I've ever known," he added, with a theatrical flourish.

On cue, a dozen patrons in the bar stood up and revealed weapons, all of which were then pointed at Griff. Before he knew what was happening, Griff's pistol had been stripped from his grasp, and his hands were cuffed behind his back.

"Meet the not-corrupt, non-asshole officers of the newly-renamed Revocater Guardian Force," said Hudson, gesturing to the group of men and women who were apprehending Griff. "They are tasked with guarding the crashed Revocater here on Earth, but we thought it fitting that they should bring you in too."

Griff struggled against the restraints, as the RGF officers conducted him towards the exit.

"This isn't over Powell!" Griff shouted, as he was bundled through the door. "You hear me? This isn't over!"

"See you around, asshole," shouted Hudson, raising his beer bottle to Griff, while Tory cockily blew him a kiss and waved him goodbye. "Maybe in, say, forty or fifty years?"

The door of the Star Scavenger's Rest slammed shut, and Hudson felt a contented peace wash over him.

"Man, that felt good," said Hudson, taking another swig of beer. It tasted suddenly blissful.

"I still say you should have let me shoot that bastard in the face," said Tory. "Figuratively speaking, of course," she added, flashing her eyes at Commodore Trent, who looked more than a little alarmed.

"So, what happens now?" asked Tobin.

"That's a question for tomorrow," answered Ma, as she refilled the glasses from the square bottle. "Tonight, we drink. Tonight, we celebrate what we saved, and honor the ones we lost."

Hudson nodded, and picked up his glass. "To Morphus," he said. The chatter between them died down, and everyone grabbed their drinks. "And to the last Revocater," Hudson added.

Then they all raised their glasses, and drank.

CHAPTER 31

Hudson stood next to Tory on the cliffs above Alamere Falls, peering out at the wrecked hulk of the last Revocater. Liberty and Tobin stood together a little off to the side, also peering out at the titanic vessel. Waves gently lapped against its hull, while a cornucopia of birds had now adopted it as a safe haven on which they could rest their wings. Hudson felt some small consolation that the ship had crashed in such a beautiful place, rather than sinking to the bottom of the ocean, forever lost. However, time hadn't dulled the sadness he still felt for the alien entity who had given everything to save them.

"It's a shame we didn't get to know Morphus better," said Hudson, "or to learn more about the people who created it."

Tory hooked her arm through Hudson's and pulled him closer. "There's still time," she said, with a hopeful tone. "The portals are still out there, and there's plenty of galaxy left to discover."

Hudson smiled at her. "You'd really want to go back out there, into the cold?" he asked. Though, when he thought about it, he wasn't surprised and he couldn't deny the idea appealed to him too.

Tory shrugged, "I somehow doubt my skillset is suited to work on this planet," she said. "And I think Trent already has me on a watch list. Besides, I want to explore."

Hudson nodded, then turned to Liberty and Tobin. "What about you two? Have you decided what comes next?" he asked.

Tobin smiled, "Well, apart from introducing Liberty to my mom," he began, to an eye roll from Liberty. "I think there's a lot of money to be made in ships right now. After all, thousands were destroyed, along with the Martian shipyards."

Liberty shook her head, and laughed. "Ever the entrepreneur – your mom would be so proud."

"I doubt it..." replied Tobin, smiling. "But think about it, some of the portal worlds survived, and will need resupplying." He turned to Liberty. "And I'll need a genius engineer to help design the new ships. Know anyone?"

Liberty shrugged, "I might... Designing and building ships doesn't come cheap, though."

This time it was Tobin who shrugged. "I guess it's a good job I'm still immensely rich then."

Hudson smiled, and reached inside his jacket, removing a crystal shard. The others all gathered round, staring at it in astonishment.

"How did you get that past Trent's new RGF Shaak scanners?" asked Tory.

Hudson patted his chest, "I have some special relic hunter tricks of my own," he said, smiling. The shielded compartment in the leather jacket that once belonged to Ericka Reach had come in useful on more than one occasion. This time, however, the relic he'd smuggled out inside the pocket wasn't intended to enrich his credit account, but rather his mental wellbeing.

Hudson slipped out Tory's knife from the scabbard on her belt, crouched down and began digging a hole into the ground. "We couldn't give Morphus a proper send off, so this is the least I could do." Hudson slid the crystal shard into the hole and covered it over. He pressed his hand to the dirt and held it there for a few seconds, before standing up. "Goodbye Morphus, and thank you," he said, humbly.

After they had all observed a few seconds of silence, Hudson spoke up again, though this time with more cheer in his voice. "There's only one more thing left to decide," he said, looking at Liberty. "If you two are going one way, and us another, who gets the Orion?"

Liberty's eyes narrowed. "You mean the VCX-110 I built with my own hands?" she said, locking her accusatory stare onto Hudson. "The one that now has a gouge cut through my favorite semi-circular sofa?"

"Erm, yeah, that one," said Hudson, shifting his feet uncomfortably.

To his surprise, Liberty smiled. "You take it; you've earned it," she said, warmly. "I can't even start the damn thing up now, anyway, after Morphus coded the ignition sequence to that alien patch in your arm." Then she glanced at Tobin, and added, "Besides, it sounds like I'm going to be designing and building something new." Then she raised her eyebrows, "And as Tobin's Vice President of Starship Design and Manufacturing, I'm sure I'll get to design a new ship of my very own, right?"

Tobin shrugged, "You're the boss, boss."

Hudson walked up to Liberty and pulled her into an embrace. "I'm going to miss you, Co-Captain Devan," he said, not wanting to let her go.

"Likewise, Co-Captain Powell," replied Liberty, returning the embrace with an even tighter hold. Then they pulled back from each other, eyes still locked together. "I know it's a big galaxy, but don't be a stranger, okay?"

Hudson nodded and backed up next to Tory. The others then said their goodbyes, Tory even managing a short, but visibly awkward hug with Liberty. Then Hudson watched as Liberty and Tobin headed back to their shuttle; one of several that Tobin owned on Earth. With Tory again at his side, Hudson continued to watch as the shuttle blasted off and rose higher into the sky.

"It's time we left too," said Tory, as the wind gusting over the cliff face toyed with her hair. "Assuming you still want to hang with an ex merc, with a temper and a slight drinking problem, that is?"

"Well, now that you put it that way..." replied Hudson, trying to suppress a grin. Then he held her shoulders and looked into her eyes. "Honestly, I can't imagine going anywhere without you."

Tory smiled and kissed Hudson, holding her lips against his for a few seconds longer than he expected.

"Don't get all soppy on me now," said Tory, as she drew back. "We're venturing into the vast unknown, so I need that tough guy relic hunter back."

"Well, you got me," said Hudson.

They walked back towards the Orion, and for some reason his father's words came into Hudson's mind again. He'd wanted him to do something that he cared about, something that mattered to him, but now, as he approached the Orion with Tory at his side, he realized he'd been chasing the wrong ideal. What mattered to him wasn't a thing. It wasn't a job or an achievement that was important, but who he was with. It was the people he cared about, and the people who cared about him. So long as he had that, he had everything he needed.

The rear ramp of the Orion clamped shut, and Hudson took the controls, lifting the ship off the cliffside and into the sky above the wrecked remains of the last Revocater. He didn't have a course set, and he didn't have a clue where he was going. He'd been a drifter for most of his adult life. He'd not known where he'd be or what he'd be doing from one month to the next. It had been his way of avoiding life; but this time it felt different. Now, as the Orion breached the atmosphere and entered into space, without a heading, he knew exactly where he belonged. He'd been a flyer, a courier runner, a guardian outcast, and a relic hunter. Now, finally, he was home.

The end.

EPILOGUE

Waves lapped against the scarred hull of the titanic vessel as it lay, half in the ocean, and half embedded into a cliff face. It did not know where it was. It remembered nothing of how it had got there. It did not recall its function. But there was one thing it did know. It knew its name. And its name was Goliath.

YOU MADE IT!

Thank you so much for reading these books. I hope you enjoyed the journey as much as I did. If you did, then please also consider reading The Contingency War Series, for Kindle and Audible.

- The Contingency
- The Waystation Gambit
- Rise of Nimrod Fleet
- Earth's Last War

"Highly recommended - sci-fi fans will not be disappointed with this novel." *Readers' Favorite, 5-star review.*

No-one comes in peace. Every being in the galaxy wants something, and is willing to take it by force...

ABOUT THE AUTHOR

At school I was asked to write down the jobs I wanted to do as a 'grown up'. Number one was astronaut and number two was a PC games journalist. I only managed to achieve one of those goals (I'll let you guess which), but these two very different career options still neatly sum up my lifelong interests in science, space and the unknown.

School also steered me in the direction of a science-focused education over literature and writing, which influenced my decision to study physics at Manchester University. What this degree taught me is that I didn't like studying physics and instead enjoyed writing, which is why you're reading this book! The lesson? School can't tell you who you are.

When not writing, I enjoy spending time with my family, walking in the British countryside, and indulging in as much Sci-Fi as possible.

You can connect with me here:
https://twitter.com/GJ_Ogden
https://www.ogdenmedia.net

Subscribe to my newsletter:
http://subscribe.ogdenmedia.net

Printed in Great Britain
by Amazon